SEEK NEW HORIZONS

Sister Dominique, already having serious doubts about her calling, is sent on a mercy mission to South America after a devastating earthquake. There, she meets Dr Steve Daniels, and feelings she had never expected to experience again are stirred up. As she is thrown into caring for a relentless stream of casualties, her thoughts are in turmoil. How will she cope in the outside world if she leaves the sisterhood? And dare she allow herself to fall in love again?

TERESA ASHBY

SEEK NEW HORIZONS

Complete and Unabridged

LINFORD
Leicester

First published in Great Britain in 1992

First Linford Edition
published 2013

A catalogue record for this book is available
from the British Library.

ISBN 978–1–4448–1682–2

Published by
F. A. Thorpe (Publishing)
Anstey, Leicestershire

Set by Words & Graphics Ltd.
Anstey, Leicestershire
Printed and bound in Great Britain by
T. J. International Ltd., Padstow, Cornwall

This book is printed on acid-free paper

1

A few hours ago, the mountains had looked beautiful, but now they had become hostile and forbidding. Low, black clouds sent snow swirling down and, with the gathering darkness, the mountains were fast becoming obscured.

She stood by the window, a small, insignificant figure with raven-coloured hair framing a pretty face. Only her pale blue eyes gave a clue to the fear which was growing within her.

She shivered, despite the warmth fanning up from the radiator. How much longer?

An hour ago, she had watched as the rescue team set out from the base, the dogs eager to get on with their work. Would Tom be angry with her for alerting the authorities about his lateness?

He'd been late from his mountaineering expeditions before, but, in the past, she'd never had this gut feeling that something was terribly wrong. Of course, she'd worried before, but, this time, no matter what she did, she couldn't quell the feeling that he wasn't coming back.

Then, out of the blizzard, she saw them coming, their luminous jackets shining like beacons in the appalling conditions.

They'd found him! Joy and relief coursed through her as she ran towards the doors of the rescue base, flinging them open and running across the snow, oblivious to the cold. Her prayers had been answered!

'No!' A burly man gripped her shoulders with a thick-gloved hand, holding her back.

'Where is he?' she wanted to know. 'Where's Tom?' Then she saw the stretcher and Tom's still form strapped to it as two men struggled to carry it through the blizzard. 'Tom!'

Wrenching herself free, she ran on, snow clinging to her hair and eyelashes, blinding her.

'I'm sorry — there's nothing you can do, love.' The burly man had his arm around her. 'Come away, lass,' he said gently. 'Come on, that's a good girl.' But she wouldn't believe it — couldn't! Not her husband! Not her Tom!

'Oh, God,' she cried, her voice thick with misery. 'Oh, God. No!'

* * *

Sister Bernadette had always had an untidy appearance, the Mother Superior thought as her Mistress of Novices entered the office. She was a tall, lean woman with a straight back and a broad smile, but somehow the younger nun always looked crumpled!

'You wanted to see me, Mother.' Sister Bernadette looked down at her superior, who was seated behind a large, handsome oak desk by the window.

'Yes, I did. Sit down, please.'

The Mother Superior quickly regretted her unkind thoughts about Sister Bernadette's appearance. Whatever she looked like, she was a fine Mistress of Novices — a hard task-master but kind and understanding to the young, future nuns in her care.

'Excuse me.' The Mother Superior smiled apologetically when the telephone rang.

Sister Bernadette moved towards the open window as the Mother Superior spoke into the telephone.

As she watched, Sister Dominique, the young nun who had transformed the flower and herb gardens, took a break from the patch she'd been weeding and surveyed her handiwork with a look of satisfaction. She had every reason to be proud, Sister Bernadette thought, after all her hard work.

But the voice of the Mother Superior suddenly cut into her thoughts.

'That was the Reverend Mother

General on the telephone. I'm afraid the latest news from South America is not at all good. There have been many more casualties from the earthquake than they first thought.'

'Those poor people. If only we could do something positive to help the victims,' Sister Bernadette sympathised.

'Perhaps we can.' The Mother Superior smiled. 'The earthquake has left many people injured and homeless. The Bishop of that area has asked the Reverend Mother General, who in turn has asked us, to provide two of our nursing Sisters to travel out there to help.'

Sister Bernadette nodded. She had seen terrible images on the television news following the earthquake, which had practically decimated an entire region.

The area was poor, with few facilities to cope with such a large-scale emergency. The people there depended largely on the services of various voluntary organisations.

'Several names spring to mind, Reverend Mother,' the Mistress of Novices said thoughtfully.

'The task will obviously require special skills. So much needs to be done,' the Mother Superior remarked sadly. 'There are whole communities to be restored, orphans to be cared for . . .'

She paused for a moment. 'It won't be an easy task. You said that several names sprung to mind?'

'Sister Dominique — working down there in the herb garden — is a shining example.' Sister Bernadette smiled expansively as she pointed through the open window to the novice nun.

'Not only is she a dedicated nun, but she's a fine nurse. And she can drive and speak fluent Spanish. Her own mother was Spanish, remember.'

'Ah!' The Mother Superior pressed her hands together on her desk and looked troubled. 'Sister Dominique!'

'Well, yes.' Sister Bernadette looked taken aback. 'You seem doubtful, Reverend Mother. Is there a problem? I know that Sister Dominique has only recently left the novitiate behind and taken profession, but . . . '

'There is a problem. Sister Dominique came to me only a few days ago and expressed some real doubts about her vocation.'

'Doubts?' Sister Bernadette looked stunned.

'Believe me, it came as a shock to me, too, but she's decidedly unsure about her future with us,' the Mother Superior went on.

'Is there a specific reason behind this?' the Mistress of Novices asked after a lengthy silence. 'I recall that when she came to us, before she had even heard her calling, that she was recovering from a personal tragedy.

'Have the circumstances which brought her to us in the first place — her husband being killed in that mountaineering accident — anything to do with her present uncertainties?'

'I'm afraid it isn't as simple as that.' The Mother Superior sighed. 'We've all had our doubts at some time or another and we've already discussed this at length . . .

'But apparently, this has been a gradual process and now she feels that she has reached a crossroads in her life.

'However, doubts or no doubts, I still feel that Sister Dominique has a tremendous amount to offer. I've thought long and hard about her situation and her fears . . . and perhaps sending her abroad will be just what she needs to help her reach a decision.

'The sheer scale of the suffering and hardship she'll witness out there will be way beyond anything she's ever seen before — minimising even her own tragedy for a time. Her faith will be stretched to its limits, tested and tried over and over again.

'At the end of it all, she'll be a stronger woman. Whether she remains a nun or not . . . ' The Mother Superior shrugged helplessly.

'We may still lose her,' Sister Bernadette said softly.

'That's the last thing I want.' The Mother Superior smiled benignly. 'All I want is for her to find the way that is right for her.

'But if God has other plans for her — and who are we to say that He hasn't — then it's not for us to stand in the way. She must make the decision herself and we can only hope that she is also guided by Him.'

Slowly she stood up and, leaning heavily on a stick, moved over to the open window and looked out on the beautiful convent gardens.

Seeing Sister Dominique out there, surrounded by peace and God's beauty, the Mother Superior came to a decision.

'Sister Bernadette,' she said firmly, 'would you please send Sister Dominique to me?'

* * *

Dominique paused for a moment to look around the tiny spartan room which had been her home for three years — the place where she had finally found some form of inner peace. A haven . . . a retreat, perhaps?

She couldn't look back over her time here without thinking of her reasons for coming in the first place.

Her world had crumbled to dust when Tom had been killed.

She closed her eyes, still able to visualise her vital, strong husband. She could almost stroke the softness of his dark hair, feel his strong arms around her, see the intense blue of his eyes.

She shuddered at the memory and opened her eyes, relief washing over her at the sight of her simple, familiar room. But, in that moment, she also realised that leaving here was going to be a dreadful wrench. It had become home and the other nuns her family.

Perhaps it would be temporary — or perhaps she would never return. She simply didn't know.

What had happened to bring about her recent doubts, she couldn't really say either. It was just a growing feeling that something was missing from her life — something vital and important.

'Are you ready, Sister Dominique?'

She jumped and turned to see Sister Magda looking round the door at her. Her bright, cheerful face was just the tonic Dominique needed to shake her from her reverie.

'Almost.' She smiled.

'Apparently we're going on an emergency supply plane.' Sister Magda grimaced. 'You and me and several boxes of urgent medical supplies! So, get your skates on. We don't want to keep the pilot waiting!'

Sister Magda hurried away and Dominique smiled, thinking that even the swish of the other nun's habit sounded happy and excited.

With a sigh, Dominique lifted her holdall from the bed and held it against her as she looked one last time around her room. Then, with a decisive step, she turned towards the door, but found her way was blocked.

'Reverend Mother!' she exclaimed and the older woman stepped inside the room, filling it at once with her presence, her aura of peace and warmth.

'I couldn't let you go without saying goodbye.' The older woman took Dominique's hands and clasped them within her own.

'I know that God will help you to find your way, Sister Dominique, and we'll all be praying for you and thinking about you.

'You have a long, difficult journey ahead of you, not just in miles, but towards a new life. You may well see and have to deal with things which will shock and confuse you. But, God willing, you'll find the strength.

'Remember, Sister, if God leads you out of the convent, it will be for a reason — that He has other plans for you.

'Above all, have faith.' The Reverend Mother smiled, then handed Dominique a book of prayers and devotions.

'Perhaps this will help you.'

'Thank you, Mother.' Dominique blinked back her tears as the Mother turned and left quietly.

She gazed down at the leather-bound breviary. As she opened it and read the hand-written dedication within, she felt a tear trace its path down her cheek.

May God help you to find your way.

Picking up her holdall, the young nun quickly left the room, without looking back . . .

But, a few moments later, when the convent door banged shut behind her and Sister Magda, she gave an involuntary start.

Suddenly, Dominique was afraid. She looked back once at the closed door and the realisation hit her like a hammer blow. She was leaving behind the life she had embraced so readily three years ago, after losing Tom.

From the safe seclusion of the convent, she was heading straight into the unknown.

2

The first thing to hit Dominique as she got off the plane was the damp, oppressive heat, which wrapped itself around her like a wet flannel, making her feel instantly uncomfortable.

She and Magda stood, side by side, on the makeshift airfield, both feeling lost as people converged on the plane, hurrying to unload the urgently-needed supplies.

'Sisters . . . uh . . . Dominique and Magda?' an American voice behind them said and they turned to see a young GI looking curiously at them.

'That's right,' Magda said, clearly relieved that they weren't to be left stranded on the airfield!

'This way, please,' the soldier said politely, reaching for their luggage and sweeping it into the back of the Jeep.

Already, the Jeep was crammed with

boxes of medical supplies and Dominique looked at it doubtfully.

'Don't worry.' The American grinned at her worried expression. 'There's plenty of room in there for two ladies.'

With little ceremony, he helped first Magda, then Dominique into the Jeep. 'Call me Chuck,' he shouted above the noise of a second supply plane which had just landed. 'Anything you need, anything at all, just ask for Chuck! Hang on, ladies!' He laughed as the vehicle bounced over the pot-holes.

'Where are we going?' Magda asked.

'We've set up camp a few miles outside the earthquake zone,' Chuck replied. 'The accommodation ain't exactly five-star, but it's the best we could do at short notice. It's not too far from here.'

After ten minutes, which felt more like an hour, of being tossed about in the Jeep, they turned a corner and came upon a clearing where khaki tents were set up around a larger, more important-looking canvas structure.

For all that, it was a wooden-framed, rather ramshackle affair — grubby white, and marked with a red cross — the hospital.

The Jeep screeched to a halt about twenty yards from it and Chuck leaped out, then held up his arms to lift both Dominique and Magda down to the ground.

People swarmed about the place, some in the uniform of American soldiers, others in white coats.

Then, from amid the chaos, an imposing figure came hurrying towards them.

'Oh, oh!' Chuck remarked. 'See ya later, folks!' Grabbing a couple of boxes from the Jeep, the GI hurried off to become part of the general confusion.

The nun bearing down on them was tall, almost statuesque and her habit blew around her like the wings of a giant bird.

She was taller than both of them and older, with a large nose and wide-set, dark eyes.

'Welcome,' she said, her voice bearing a trace of an Italian accent. 'I am Sister Augusta. You must be Sisters Magda and Dominique. I hope you're not too exhausted after your journey.

'I'm in overall charge of the hospital,' Sister Augusta explained, motioning the two Sisters to follow her, 'and I do my best to co-ordinate the efforts of the various organisations at work here.'

She swung around then and walked quickly towards the hospital.

'This is our main hospital,' she explained as she led them inside.

They followed the Sister through the tent. 'In there is the operating theatre and, beyond that, the emergency treatment room.'

Dominique looked around her. The patients ranged from old men to tiny babies. Some of them were obviously gravely ill, others were able to walk around, and those who could eyed the two new arrivals curiously.

'This is Luis Garcia.' Sister Augusta introduced them to an elderly man.

Dominique spoke to him in fluent Spanish, asking how he was feeling.

The old man was plainly delighted to be spoken to in his own language and let forth a flood of rapid Spanish which left Sister Augusta baffled.

'Sister Dominique's mother was Spanish,' Magda whispered to Sister Augusta. 'The language is as natural to her as English.'

Dominique held his hand and he spoke softly, tears filling his eyes.

'That's the first time that man has spoken since he was brought here,' Sister Augusta commented when they eventually moved away. 'He's been in deep shock.

'That's undoubtedly a valuable asset you have there, being able to speak the language of the country. Well done, Sister Dominique.'

Dominique smiled modestly, then felt her attention straying when she saw a small, dark boy watching her from behind a curtain. When he saw her, he ducked shyly out of the way.

Dominique turned back to what Sister Augusta was saying, but suddenly felt the faintest whisper of a touch on her skin. She looked down to see the little boy who had been watching her, now standing at her side.

He was about six years old, skinny and small — olive skinned, with a large sticking plaster dangling from a healing graze on his chin. His mop of dark hair only added to his persona of a street urchin.

'This is Pedro,' Sister Augusta explained. 'He suffered only superficial injuries in the earthquake, but, tragically, lost all his family.

'The only reason that he is alive today is because he was in school, not at home, when the earthquake struck.

'I should warn you that he isn't as angelic as he looks,' she added with a wry smile, sensing at once that Dominique was quite smitten. 'He needs to be watched very carefully indeed that one!'

Dominique looked down at little

Pedro again, her heart contracting when she thought of all he had been through in his young life.

Suddenly he tugged his hand free and ran away and Sister Dominique heard Sister Magda ask, 'Is there anyone here responsible for our spiritual needs? I understand that the mission was destroyed.'

Sister Augusta's mouth tightened into a thin line and she replied, rather abruptly, 'The mission was ruined but Father Gomez will take confession. I suppose you had better meet him.'

'Oh!' Dominique cried out as Sister Augusta headed outside.

'What is it?' the older Sister demanded, stopping in her tracks and looking down at the young woman, with hawk-like, black eyes.

'My rosary!' Dominique, bewildered and confused, looked from Magda to Sister Augusta. 'It's gone! I — I must have dropped it somewhere.

'I know I had it with me when we came into the hospital. I remember showing it to Señor Garcia.'

In despair, she looked on the floor, but Sister Augusta was already marching purposefully over to Pedro.

He was sitting on the end of one of the beds and turned slowly to look at her as she approached, his beautiful, wide eyes round and appealing.

She said nothing, just held out her hand, palm upwards.

The child looked sheepish, then reached into the pocket of his ragged trousers, withdrawing Dominique's rosary, a broad grin lighting up his face.

'I wasn't going to keep it,' he said in Spanish. 'I only meant to borrow it.'

He dropped it into Sister Augusta's outstretched hand and she closed her fingers around it, firmly.

Wordlessly, she handed it back to Dominique, then swept out of the hospital and strode past the numerous tents and wooden shacks.

'This is where you will find Father Gomez — most of the time.' Sister Augusta indicated a shabby tent set apart from the rest. She stepped forward, rapping sharply on the wooden door-frame.

Almost at once, an elderly woman pushed aside the flap. Her black hair was peppered with silver and heavy bags hung beneath her eyes.

'We wish to see Father Gomez — at once,' Sister Augusta said sharply.

'The Father, he is resting,' Maria, his housekeeper, told them indignantly.

'He will see us!' Sister August announced confidently and strode past, forcing Maria to one side.

The tent was gloomy inside, lit only by two flickering, burned-down candles.

Dominique thought she heard the Sister sigh as their eyes fell upon the priest, slumped over an old wooden table, his head resting on one arm. The other arm was out of sight. She caught her superior's look of disapproval.

'Poor Father Gomez,' Magda whispered. 'He's obviously exhausted.'

'He probably hasn't slept for days,'

Dominique added. 'There's been so much to do here. I wonder if he's even taken the time to eat.'

'We — we shouldn't disturb him,' Magda said hesitantly and began to back away. 'We can come back another time when the Father's feeling more rested.'

But their whispered voices disturbed the dozing priest, who then stirred, dropping the empty whisky bottle which he had been holding in his hidden hand!

It rolled across the wooden floor, the clink of glass almost ear-splitting in the sudden, shocked silence, before finally coming to rest against the leg of a chair.

For a moment, all three nuns were too stunned to say or do anything, then Sister Augusta took charge and began ushering the two younger Sisters from the tent.

'He isn't exhausted at all,' she exclaimed angrily. 'He's drunk! And he's supposed to be guiding us spiritually. This matter will have to be dealt with properly!'

With that, she stormed from the tent.

* * *

It was uncharacteristically cool in the early morning and the nuns, volunteers from all over the world, had gathered in their makeshift chapel for Mass. Though dressed in an assortment of practical outfits, ranging from combat gear to the habits of the more traditional orders, their devotions were, nonetheless, solemn and heartfelt.

The only light in the hastily-erected building was from the candles which bathed the nuns in a soft glow.

Gentle voices lifted in worship and for those passing outside, the hymn, sung in Latin, sounded like the song of an angelic choir.

As Dominique kneeled in prayer, she realised the ground had begun to shudder beneath her feet. The sensation lasted only a few seconds but the distant rumbling noise, like far-off thunder, continued a few seconds longer.

A wooden cross fell to the ground and a plaster statue of the Holy Mother shattered into a thousand fragments on the floor.

Dominique watched it in horror and, looking at the other nuns, saw the confusion in their eyes, too. But even then she didn't realise quite what had happened until the door flew open and a doctor rushed in.

'There've been more tremors! We need your help, Sisters — now!'

Sister Augusta swept towards the door, the nuns following obediently in her wake.

The doctor was already running back towards the hospital where others waited, looking out along the uneven road which led to the devastated town.

'Harriet!' Sister Augusta moved among them, picking people out. 'Take two of your nurses and go into the earthquake zone. Your skills will be needed.'

'Chuck, you drive them.'

It was a long time since Dominique had been a casualty nurse. She prayed she hadn't forgotten anything she had learned.

'Listen!' Magda said fearfully. 'What's that noise?'

'That's the first of the casualties arriving,' Sister Augusta said quietly, crossing herself, and, seconds later, three army ambulances screeched to a halt, sending up a cloud of dust.

The first casualty was lifted out and laid on the ground and Dominique felt a rush of pity when she saw he was only young — her own age, perhaps even younger.

She touched his face gently and, as he turned to look at her, memories of her own personal tragedy flooded her mind. If only there had been someone on hand to share her Tom's last hours.

'La enfermera . . . ' he pleaded, using the Spanish for nurse. Dominique was wearing a simple white outfit, even her crucifix was hidden beneath her blouse.

Gently, she lifted his hand in her own, careful not to add to his pain. 'La monja,' she told him and his tormented features relaxed slightly as Dominique began to pray.

The noise and chaos all around seemed to fade and become distant. Now that he knew that she was a nun, the fear in his eyes began to recede.

He gazed up at her, as his fingers tightened around her own. With her free hand she touched his face again.

'Don't be afraid,' she whispered, speaking in his own language, her voice soothing.

Suddenly, Dominique felt a weight on her shoulder and was spun round forcibly by a large, strong hand.

Before she could either protest or explain, the hand had shoved her roughly aside and a voice was shouting, 'Come along, nurse! There's no time for that! We have to look after the living. Perhaps there's a chance that we may save this man — unless you want him to die!'

Dominique pressed her hand to her lips to silence her own audible shock as the doctor turned his back on her and began to bellow at the orderlies.

'Get this man to the theatre! And get a blood match — NOW! There's no time to lose.'

Then, he turned back briefly to look at Dominique and caught her completely off guard. His eyes were so penetrating — as if they could reach out and touch her very soul.

She'd never seen such eyes, since Tom . . .

3

She felt herself knocked aside as the orderlies rushed past carrying the young man away on a stretcher.

She wanted to say something in her own defence to this man but, before she could utter a sound, the young doctor had brushed past her, dashing to keep up with the flood of victims pouring into the hospital.

All around her people were rushing to and from the ambulances, shouting instructions, the injured crying out for help.

She had failed already! She should have made sure that patient was taken immediately into the emergency room. But, for a moment, she had been just a nun, not a nurse.

A wave of dizziness swept over her as the intense heat of the day began to settle around her. She felt lost already

— more lost than she'd ever been in her life.

'Nurse! Over here.'

She answered the call automatically, running to take a small child in her arms. The infant was wrapped in a blanket and, as she hurried towards the hospital, that same deep American voice that had already admonished her exploded behind her.

'No, nurse! That one's for the morgue!'

'Oh, please God, no,' she whispered, forcing back the foul taste which rose up in her throat. Death was no stranger to her, but this was just a small child!

And, in that instant, she was sure of only one thing — and that was the Reverend Mother's awful mistake in sending her to this place.

Her faith would never stand the test!

★　★　★

Having poured herself the last of the coffee from a metal pot, Sister Domin- ique collapsed gratefully into a chair in the small ante-room within the main hospital tent.

It was late afternoon and she felt weary and exhausted. Looking around, she saw that everyone else seemed to be in the same state.

Her hand shook as she raised her tin mug to her lips and she had to use her other hand to hold it steady.

The coffee was cold and strong, but she swallowed the liquid quickly, barely tasting it.

No wonder she was tired. The long journey to South America, the intense heat, and then the emergency which had heralded her first morning on duty at the makeshift hospital had all taken their toll.

This was the first break of the day for the medical team of which she was a part.

For a long while no-one spoke. Everyone seemed lost in a world of their own.

Although she was aware that she was the only nun in the room, she didn't stand out from the rest as all the nurses were dressed the same. No-one else knew yet.

Dominique had become part of the team in the operating theatre, assisting none other than the doctor who had cut her down so sharply earlier in the day.

His name, she had learned, was Steve Daniels and as she watched him work in the operating theatre, her wariness of him quickly turned to admiration.

'How did the Caesarean go, Lisa?' Dr Daniels asked the other young American doctor who was wearily rubbing her eyes.

'No problem.' Lisa Wayne's face lit up. 'Two healthy girls — and they're going to be named Lisa and Magda!'

'Fame at last.' Dr Daniels grinned.

Dominique was equally pleased for her companion, Sister Magda, who had trained as a midwife before entering the Sisterhood.

'You didn't do so badly yourself, Steve,' Lisa Wayne remarked. 'I hear you've probably saved a child's foot.'

Several pairs of tired eyes turned admiringly to look at Steve Daniels. Everyone knew how hard he'd worked on that little girl, not least Dominique, who had assisted throughout the four-hour operation.

Then they all fell silent again — even the effort of conversation proved too much.

Dominique looked at Lisa Wayne. Her long, blonde hair was pulled back quite severely from her pale, pretty face, but the few tendrils that had escaped helped to soften her image.

For someone who looked so fragile, Lisa Wayne was surprisingly tough.

'Any more coffee in that pot, nurse?' Lisa stood and stretched her long tanned arms.

'Oh, I'm sorry,' Dominique said quickly, 'I think I've finished it.'

'Don't worry about it.' Lisa smiled and sat down again. 'I probably wouldn't have the strength to drink it anyway! Besides, I saw you in the operating tent, working with the slave-driver here. You probably need it more than I do!'

'Slave-driver?' Steve Daniels laughed. 'I've been called a lot of things, but that's a new one!'

Dominique looked at him again. Her first impression — that he was extremely good-looking — had been accurate, but she had to admit she had completely misjudged his character from their initial encounter.

As she had watched him at work in the operating theatre, she had seen another side to him. The tireless way he worked, the compassion and gentle consideration he showed whether he was performing major surgery or stitching an injured finger.

The doctor hadn't even realised who she was at first as she assisted at the operation on a young man with horrific chest injuries. But when he did, he'd smiled gently at her and whispered encouragingly, 'I think he's going to make it.'

No sooner had he finished operating on the young man, than a child was brought in requiring urgent attention.

'I'll need your help again, nurse,' he'd addressed Dominique. 'Are you up to it? Not feeling faint or anything?'

'I'll be fine,' she'd said firmly.

The frightened little girl who'd been brought in, her foot twisted at an unnatural angle from being trapped for too long in the rubble that had been her home, was soothed by the doctor's gentle voice as he carried her to the operating table.

'Hey, anyone here speak Spanish? How do I tell her she's going to be OK?' He looked around.

Dominique cleared her throat and uttered a few words in Spanish. He'd stared at her for a moment, then looked down at the little girl and ruffled her hair.

'Hear what the nurse says? You're gonna be just fine, honey.' He'd grinned at Dominique. 'Thanks, nurse! I guess you said it all for me.'

Again Dominique found herself feeling thoroughly disconcerted when he'd stared straight at her with those penetrating blue eyes.

Once the child was anaesthetised he took over. 'OK, guys, let's get to it!'

After, he'd proceeded to work for four solid hours repairing the damaged tissue as best he could.

He groaned when he'd finished, a look of anguish in his eyes. 'I just hope we've fixed that foot. The kid deserves a break after all she's been through.'

Now Dominique glanced at him and felt a wave of admiration for the dedicated, young doctor.

His eyes were heavy and bloodshot and his shoulders were stooped with fatigue.

'Well, if that's it for now, folks, I suggest we all try to get some sleep,' Steve Daniels said wearily.

Even as he spoke there was another interruption.

'Doctor Daniels!'

Dr Lansing, the senior surgeon in the

makeshift hospital rushed into the room. He was a short man, in his early fifties, with dark hair turning grey and kind, gentle eyes.

'It's that chest wound, I'm afraid,' Dr Lansing said. 'It looks like you'll have to go in again, Steve. The guy's blood pressure's dropping fast . . . '

'Haemorrhage. Damn!' Steve Daniels jumped to his feet. 'Just what I was hoping to avoid.'

'I've another emergency on my hands,' the senior surgeon said, 'or I'd step in to help you sort it out.'

'I'll do this one for you, Steve,' Lisa Wayne volunteered. 'You're shattered.'

'No. I'm fine, Lisa, thanks.' Steve Daniels looked over at Dominique. 'Nurse, come with me. I think this one's special to you, too.' He touched the young nun's shoulder and hurried towards the operating theatre.

'It's not looking good, Doctor Daniels.' The theatre sister's expression was serious.

Wordlessly, Steve and Dominique put

on fresh gowns and scrubbed up.

'Sure you're up to this, nurse?' There was already a thin film of perspiration on Steve's upper lip as Dominique nodded. 'Right, let's get this show on the road.'

The combination of no food and exhaustion made Dominique feel very light-headed, but she forced herself to concentrate.

Another thought entered her head as she watched the swift, skilful way Steve Daniels worked . . . if anyone can save him, he can. She forced herself to be optimistic.

Finding the source of the bleeding seemed to take for ever and was complicated by the amount of blood the patient was losing.

'Got it! Nurse, clamp here . . . good girl! Steady . . . Hold it!'

Dominique held tightly to the clamp, watching as the doctor expertly repaired a tear no bigger than a shirt button.

'Blood pressure rising,' someone said

at last and Dominique felt a wave of relief wash over her.

'OK, ease it off now.' The doctor took the clamp from Dominique. 'You OK? You did really well.' He grinned. 'I'm proud of you!'

A little later, once Dr Daniels was sure his patient's condition was stable, he and Dominique left together to get cleaned up.

'I like the way you worked in there, nurse,' he congratulated her. 'You stayed cool even when the pressure was on — that's what I like. And I'd like to have you working with me in future.'

'Thank you.' Dominique flushed, not expecting praise. 'I'd like that.'

'Good, that's settled then.' He grinned, showing his even white teeth. 'Glad to have you aboard! By the way, I've been meaning to apologise to you all day, but I haven't had the chance.'

'Apologise?' Dominique looked up at him, wide-eyed.

'For yelling at you this morning. I didn't realise you were new to all this and it takes some getting used to. Things were pretty hectic then, though. I hope you'll forgive me.'

'Of course!' Dominique smiled, relieved. All day she'd been wondering if, in some way, she was to blame for the unhappy episode earlier.

'I guess you'll have gathered by now, I'm Steve Daniels.' He grinned boyishly and held out his hand.

Dominique shook it firmly.

'Sister Dominique,' she said, smiling back. 'I'm on Sister Augusta's team!'

She introduced herself properly for the first time, watching as surprise registered in his eyes at the revelation that she was a nun.

Later, after a brief rest period, Dominique was back on duty in the hospital.

It was evening, but the sun was still strong enough to penetrate the thick canvas of the hospital tent and cast a warm glow inside.

Most of the patients were sleeping. She moved quietly between the rows of beds and checked the blood pressure of the young man who had undergone emergency surgery earlier.

Confidently she noted down the near normal reading. He was yet to regain consciousness, but everything was looking hopeful.

Moving on, she was aware of a dark-eyed little boy watching her, the sheets pulled right up to his chin.

'Why are you still awake?' she asked softly, trying not to smile.

As she straightened the covers, she noticed a little toy donkey tucked into bed beside him.

'Who's this?' she asked, lapsing into Spanish. She tickled its ears.

'It's Rico. A lady from the village makes them,' Pedro explained, giving the donkey a fierce, possessive hug.

'He's very sweet.' Dominique smiled gently at the boy. 'But you should be sleeping by now.'

'Can't.' Pedro grinned cheekily.

'Why not?' Dominique patted his pillow. 'Aren't you comfortable, Pedro?'

'Susanna keeps crying.' He pointed to a dark-eyed, tearful little girl opposite. 'She's sad. She wants her Mama,' Pedro explained and, for the first time, Dominique saw sadness in his dark eyes.

Dominique patted Pedro's hand. 'Don't you worry, Pedro. I'll take care of her.'

She made to move away.

'Wait!' Pedro tugged the little donkey out from beneath his covers. 'Give him to Susanna — he will make her feel better.'

She took the donkey and gazed down at the little boy. His eyelids were heavy now. She touched his cheek, marvelling at the velvety softness of his skin.

'Sleep now, Pedro,' she said softly, gently stroking his head until his eyes closed.

He had been misjudged, she thought, as she hurried over to the bed in the corner. There was more to him than the light-fingered little scamp everyone seemed to think he was.

'Susanna,' she said softly and the little girl turned to look up at her with anguished eyes. Her pillow was wet with tears and she held out her skinny arms to Dominique.

'There, there.' Dominique hugged her and stroked her hair.

Then, tilting Susanna's chin, she wiped away the child's tears.

'Look, Susanna, Pedro wants you to have this.'

At once, Susanna's eyes lit up and she grabbed the donkey and held it close, momentarily comforted. And when Dominique left her a few minutes later, she was comforted and sleeping peacefully.

Dominique was glad to be off duty at midnight and, as she left the hospital tent, she bumped into Chuck, the friendly GI who'd picked them up at the airport. Chuck was the sort who could be relied on to get hold of anything and everything from bottles of Scotch to video cameras. She noticed right away that he held several toy

43

donkeys in his arms.

'Evening, Sister,' he called in greeting. 'Guess you haven't noticed any stray donkeys wandering around?'

'I can't say I have, Chuck, why?' At the same time, she was feeling the first twinge of suspicion.

'You can't trust anybody these days,' he grumbled, gripping a short cigar between his teeth. 'I had six of these little beauties specially made by one of the locals — and some . . . um . . . somebody's lifted one!'

'Lifted, Chuck?'

'Yeah, like stolen!'

Dominique's astonishment quickly turned to amusement.

'Oh, I wouldn't worry too much. Your donkey's probably being treasured by someone even as we speak!'

'Yeah,' Chuck mumbled. 'Sure, Sister.'

He shrugged resignedly and wandered off, still muttering under his breath, leaving Dominique smiling to herself.

4

Dominique still felt exhausted the following morning, but at the same time she was eager to get to the hospital to help.

For the first time in so long, she felt as though her life really had some meaning. Then, as she and Sister Magda left for the hospital, Sister Augusta stopped them.

'I'm glad to have this opportunity to speak to you both.

'I didn't have the chance to speak to you yesterday, but I understand that you both coped admirably.

'I had hoped to ease you in here a little more gently.' She sighed. 'But in a situation of such magnitude everything is unpredictable . . . '

'Thank you, Sister.' Magda smiled. 'May we be excused now? Sister Dominique and I both wish to see

Father Gomez to make our confession.'

At the mention of his name, Sister Augusta's mouth tightened in disapproval.

'Go ahead,' she said at last. As Dominique and Magda hurried away, they heard her muttering to herself, 'Something must be done about that man! He's a disgrace to the Church!'

Dominique would have liked to have asked Magda what she thought of Sister Augusta's outburst, but there was no time before they reached the Father's tent.

Maria, Father Gomez's Spanish housekeeper, pulled aside the flap and glared at the two Sisters, then her face relaxed into a smile.

'Is Father Gomez here?' Dominique asked politely.

'He is gone,' Maria said gesticulating vaguely. 'Where is the black crow?'

Both nuns pretended not to know who Maria was talking about.

'You come in.' Maria ushered them into the tent. 'Sit, sit. I tell you the truth of what happen. Father Gomez, he is not a . . . ' She screwed up her face as she searched for the right words in English.

'Would it be easier if we spoke in Spanish?' Dominique asked kindly and Maria nodded.

Magda raised an eyebrow.

'I'll tell you later what she says,' Dominique promised.

'The Father likes to have a drink occasionally,' Maria explained, calmer now, 'but what you saw yesterday . . . well . . . there was a reason.'

'Take your time, Maria.' Dominique leaned forward and squeezed the housekeeper's hand.

Maria twisted a handkerchief between her fingers as she spoke brokenly.

'If it had not been for Esteban . . . poor Esteban.' Maria dabbed at tears which welled up in her eyes.

'Tell me about Esteban,' Dominique pressed gently.

'A month before the earthquake, Father Gomez married Esteban to his childhood sweetheart, Rosamunda. They were so happy together, Sister.

'Everyone in the village was happy for them, but when the earthquake came, Rosamunda was killed.'

Maria's voice quivered and she took a few moments to compose herself.

'She was such a bright, beautiful girl . . . full of life. Esteban is so full of anger. He can't seem to come to terms with his loss. He would not even go to her funeral . . . as if by not doing so he can deny her death.

'Since then all he seems to do is drink . . . the Father's tried his best to comfort him, but he's inconsolable.'

She took a deep breath.

'He says drinking eases the pain — so that he does not have to think — or remember.

'So, Father Gomez stays with him, also drinking!

' ''What can I say to ease that young man's grief?' he asks me, when eventually he comes back. He was so dejected at being unable to help

Esteban that he finished what was left in the bottle.

'He was so tired, Sister, and there had been too many funerals that day. He's barely slept at all since the tragedy.

'You saw him at his worst. You did not see the real Father Gomez.'

Love and admiration shone in her eyes.

'He is a good man, a good priest. Sister Augusta does not know him as I do. I hope you will try to understand.'

Dominique was touched by Maria's loyalty.

'Thank you, Maria. Father Gomez is lucky to have you. Of course we understand. We knew that there must be an explanation for what happened.

'We have to leave now, but we'll come back another time to see the Father.'

'Thank you, Sisters, from the bottom of my heart.' Maria spoke in English again. 'I will tell Father Gomez that you were here.'

'You don't have to look so disappointed, Sister Magda,' Dominique said when she'd repeated everything that Maria had told her.

'I'm not disappointed,' Magda protested. 'But a drunken priest would have made life more interesting, especially with Sister Augusta in charge of things, don't you think?'

'You're terrible!' Dominique laughed. 'And I don't believe you mean a word of it.'

'Sister Magda,' someone was calling and Magda hurried towards one of the civilian nurses.

'One of the women in the village has gone into labour and she's still refusing to come to the hospital. Chuck's waiting in the Jeep to take you to her, but you'll have to hurry!'

Dominique watched her go, then made her way to the hospital.

The rota for the day was pinned up in the ante-room and, thinking everyone had gone, Dominique went to check it. Suddenly, she heard Lisa

Wayne's voice. She murmured something. Then she laughed and Dominique saw Steve Daniels pulling her into his arms, lowering his head to kiss her.

Dominique drew back, unable to understand why her heart was hammering so fast. The last thing she wanted was to be caught spying but, suddenly and unaccountably, she felt rooted to the spot.

The sound of Lisa's laughter galvanised her into action and she headed back into the ward, deciding that she could check the rota later, knowing only that she had to get away.

These sudden, strange, unfamiliar feelings frightened her and she was loathe to admit, even to herself, that these confusing emotions were uncommonly like jealousy . . .

★ ★ ★

'Sister Dominique, I have nine now!' Pedro ran to Dominique and held a box under her nose. Cockroaches!

'Well done, Pedro! The fewer of them we have, the better,' Dominique said encouragingly. 'Now take them and release them outside — but not too close to the hospital!'

She watched him run away and smiled. He needed something to keep him occupied and catching insects seemed to be the ideal solution. As he ran towards the door, he collided with the priest coming in.

Dominique hurried forward as the Father steadied Pedro with his hands.

'Not so fast, Pedro!' Father Gomez laughed. 'Always in a hurry, aren't you?'

Then Pedro insisted on showing his box of insects to the Father before dashing outside.

'Your idea?' The priest raised his eyebrows at Dominique and she nodded.

'Yes.' His smile widened. 'Perhaps that's the answer to curbing the scamp's mischievousness . . . if Pedro has something to occupy him . . . ' His voice trailed away and Dominique couldn't help thinking that there was a depth of sorrow in the man's eyes that she hadn't noticed until now.

'But I haven't come here to disturb you, nurse. I realise how busy you all are. I wonder if you could tell me where I may find Sister Dominique or Sister Magda.'

'Father Gomez, I am Sister Dominique.'

'Ah!' He beamed. 'I was hoping to find you here. I'm sorry I was out when you came to see me. And I apologise for the circumstances of our first meeting.'

'Please, don't worry,' Dominique said gently. 'You must have been very tired.'

She felt uncomfortable at the Father's obvious embarrassment and quickly changed the subject.

'I was hoping you'd hear my confession, Father.'

'Of course, Sister. If you'd like to come with me, I'll hear it now — if it's convenient.'

Dominique quickly explained to one of the other nurses where she would be, then rejoined the Father.

They walked together to the Father's tent and Dominique found him surprisingly easy to get along with.

He was much younger than she'd first thought.

His dark hair was cut severely short, but his features remained kind and good-humoured.

'You've had a rather harsh introduction to life out here, I understand,' he said. 'A lot of the doctors and nurses are experienced in working under these emergency conditions. Everyone is so dedicated.

'The best advice I can offer you,' he added, leading her towards his tent, 'is to keep your sense of humour.'

They had hardly entered the tent, when the flap was wrenched aside and a young man rushed in.

Dominique recoiled in fear. His eyes were wild and angry and the strong smell of alcohol from his breath was overpowering.

He was unshaven and his unruly

black hair looked as if it hadn't been combed for days.

'Esteban . . . ' Father Gomez lifted his hand to calm the young man, but he was beyond reason.

'Why is my Rosamunda dead?' he shouted, desperately. 'What kind of God,' he implored, 'takes young women and little children?'

'Esteban.' Father Gomez reached out a comforting hand to touch the young man's arm, but Esteban wrenched himself away roughly and his eyes flashed with hatred.

'There is no God!' he yelled. 'The kind and loving God you preach about does not exist!'

Dominique was stunned. All the things he was saying were the same things she herself had thought when Tom was killed.

Like Esteban, she had not been married for very long. Like Esteban, she couldn't understand why God had taken the one she loved.

She knew exactly how he felt, how

desperate and confused, and she longed to reach out and help him.

'God's testing your faith, Esteban,' she murmured softly, slipping easily into Spanish.

He looked at her, startled.

'God would never have taken your wife without good reason.'

Esteban's mouth fell open and he glared at Dominique, unsure of how to react in the face of her quiet assurance.

'What do you mean?' he sneered defiantly.

'You can rant and rave all you like, it won't bring her back. She is with God now — at rest, at peace. It's time for you to find peace within yourself and now only He can help you do that.'

Dominique's voice shook, but her resolve remained firm.

'I know what it's like to lose someone you love . . . someone you expected to spend your whole life with . . .

'It hurts, Esteban — I know — it is the most painful thing in the world, but you will survive. God has spared you, as he has me.

'Open your heart and listen to Him,' she went on. 'And tell Him of your doubts and fears. God does nothing without reason.

'He changed my life because it was His wish that I became a nun. Please, Esteban, I beg you, listen to what God has to tell you.'

Maria had come into the tent, a basket of provisions in her arms. The young man looked from Father Gomez to Dominique and the anger in his eyes faded. Now he looked confused as he pressed his fingers against his forehead.

'I — I'm sorry, Father. I . . . '

'Come.' Maria put her arm around him and led him outside. 'I will take you home and get you some food. How long since you ate? Look at you, all skin and bone!'

'You spoke from the heart, Sister,' Father Gomez said gratefully when Maria and Esteban had gone. 'He knew that and that's why he listened.

'I have been so busy telling him to remember the good times, that I neglected to consider the future.

'Thank you, Sister. You said all the right things just now and I'm grateful.'

He looked at the young nun and saw that she herself looked drained and pale. Why, when she had managed to reach Esteban where he had failed?

If he didn't know better, he'd say she looked guilty and very unhappy.

'What's troubling you, Sister Dominique?'

She looked up at him, her eyes brimming with tears and when she spoke, her voice was subdued and faltering.

'You're right, Father,' she said shakily. 'I may have said all the right things to Esteban, but, God forgive me, I'm not sure I believe any of it myself any more.

'Father, I'm so confused. I just don't know what to believe.'

The Father's mouth was dry. He stared at the young nun, saw the conflict raging inside her, and his heart ached for her.

There was nothing he could do or say to resolve her obvious doubts. It was something she had to face herself.

'The way will become clear,' Father Gomez said, knowing that his words were hopelessly inadequate as far as this young nun was concerned.

Dominique sensed it, too.

'Will it?' she said miserably. 'Will it ever?'

Father Gomez pulled a rickety wooden chair out from under the table. He was troubled by Sister Dominique's revelation and anxious to help.

'Sit down, please, Sister. We need to talk . . . ' he said gently.

Dominique was trembling visibly as she sank on to the chair and her cheeks were flushed.

What little she had said was enough to confirm that her doubts were grave and deep-rooted.

As the priest pulled out another chair for himself he looked long and hard at

Dominique, searching for some clues as to the cause of her recent unhappiness.

'Do you think your doubts arise from the loss of your loved one?' he coaxed gently.

Dominique sighed and shook her head.

'If only it were as simple as that, Father,' she said. 'If anything, the misery and uncertainty I felt after Tom's . . . my husband's death, led me to seek the answers to so many questions — led me into the Sisterhood in fact.

'That's where I'm so different from Esteban. His loss has taken him away from God — mine brought me closer to Him . . . '

She paused for a moment, trying to think of a way to explain her feelings.

'I can't explain, Father. It's nothing tangible. Perhaps if there was a solid reason, it would be easier, but there isn't.'

'I think you're being too hard on yourself, Sister Dominique. Most of us, as you know already, have had doubts at some stage. With God's help, you'll work through this crisis just as we all have — of that I'm sure.'

Dominique nodded. His reassuring words had a calming effect on her as she realised they had almost echoed her Mother Superior's words back home in England.

Father Gomez let go of her hands and as Dominique smiled shyly he was relieved to see her serenity return.

'Feel free to come to me at any time to discuss your worries,' he said warmly.

'Thank you, Father,' she said. 'You're very kind and don't worry too much about Esteban. If he'd like to talk again any time . . . I'll be happy to listen.'

'I'm sure you will,' the priest replied softly. 'With you, I think, Sister Dominique, it is not your faith you doubt, but your calling — that much is clear to me already. Now, if you're ready, I'll hear your confession.'

Dominique lowered her eyes, placed

her hands together in her lap and began to speak softly.

'Forgive me, Father, for I have sinned . . .'

★   ★   ★

The two doctors had driven into the small town nearest the hospital on their first evening off since they'd joined the emergency operation — and were looking for somewhere to eat.

They stopped outside a crumbling building incongruous with coloured lights strung up outside and soft music coming from within.

'This looks possible,' Steve Daniels suggested. 'Wanna take a quick look?'

Lisa Wayne looked slightly apprehensive, but she nodded.

'Buenos tardes, Señor!' Steve smiled broadly as he entered the posada and addressed the owner.

'Are you still open for business?'

'Buenos tardes. Of course we're open! It will take more than an earthquake to put Diego Martino out of business!' The owner introduced himself with a short bow. 'And I assure you, Señorita,' he said noticing Lisa's wariness, 'the building is perfectly safe.'

'A table for two, then, please — if you have one.' Steve grinned.

Señor Martino gestured expansively. 'Come this way, please.'

He led them past several tables, attractively laid with red cloths and bowls of white flowers, to a more intimate one in the corner.

Lisa still looked nervous as they sat down and gasped when they glanced up and saw the sky above.

'Just a small hole,' Señor Martino smiled broadly, handing them each a menu. 'Pablo will serve you.'

'That's a small hole?' Lisa laughed incredulously.

'It is,' Steve said, poker-faced, 'compared to that one.'

Lisa looked up again and saw a gaping hole in the roof. The more they looked around, the more damage from the earthquake they saw. Sticky tape held the glass in the windows and large splinters of wood hung from the ceiling like cobwebs.

Pablo, the young waiter, smiled welcomingly as he lit the candles on the table and took their order.

Smiling, Steve picked up the bottle of wine and filled Lisa's glass.

She sat gazing up at the sky above her. 'This is fantastic, Steve,' she murmured. 'Look, there must be a thousand stars up there. It's so romantic . . . '

'It is, isn't it?' Steve enthused. 'I can't believe we're actually having a night off! A chance to relax and talk about something else besides broken legs and blood transfusions!'

'I'm glad you suggested we take a chance and come to town tonight, Steve.' Lisa smiled dreamily.

'We'll have to come here again,' he said.

Lisa sighed happily. 'Once we're married, Steve, we'll have lots of evenings like this. Just us, darling . . . '

She carried on talking, but Steve heard none of it. Suddenly his appetite had vanished and his stomach was in knots. Had he heard right?

She had mentioned marriage, hadn't she? With a jolt, he realised that she was still talking about the future, their future . . .

Obviously, somewhere along the line, Lisa had read more into their relationship than he had intended. Surely he'd never done or said anything to give her that idea?

Lisa was a lovely girl and he thought the world of her, but marriage — to her or anyone else — was something he'd never seriously considered.

As she talked, he wondered how on earth he was going to break it to her that his plans for the future didn't coincide with hers. The last thing he wanted to do was hurt her.

The rest of the evening went by in a haze for Steve.

Suddenly, he got up from the table

and beckoned to Pablo to bring the bill. Lisa stared up at him in surprise, then smiled tolerantly. She understood how dedicated he was.

'We really should be getting back, Lisa,' he said. 'I'd like to take another look at a couple of patients before I turn in.'

'OK, I understand, Steve,' she said, getting up. 'It's been a long day anyway.'

Steve turned away guiltily as he paid the bill. He really did like Lisa but . . . as a friend . . . not as his future wife. If only she wasn't so nice . . .

5

'Are you still here, Sister Dominique?' The young nurse tapped Dominique on the shoulder. 'Don't you know the time?'

Dominique looked up gratefully from the temperature chart she was filling in.

'Thanks. My watch is broken and I didn't realise the time.

'I think it must have got broken during that first emergency. I really miss it. You don't know anyone who could fix it?'

A little way away, Pedro, the little orphan boy whom she had befriended, sat at a small table, coaxing the little girl, Susanna, to eat.

She was gazing at him trustingly with huge dark eyes, the donkey he had given her tucked permanently under her arm.

But Pedro's mind was no longer on

persuading Susanna to eat as he got up from the table and headed outside.

Outside the hospital, a group of GIs were unloading a Jeep. Pedro watched them, listening to their cheerful banter for a moment before picking Chuck out and swaggering confidently up to him.

'Hiya, kid!' Chuck grinned at the boy and ruffled his black hair. 'How're you doing?'

Pedro spoke some English, but he rarely let on just how much he knew.

'We talk,' he said, his cherubic face serious as he tugged at Chuck's jacket, leading him away from the Jeep.

Intrigued, Chuck went along with him. He knew a little Spanish himself, taught to him by his Mexican immigrant mother, but hardly enough to hold a proper conversation.

'You have watches?' Pedro asked bluntly. 'Good ones, no barato.' He tapped his wrist. 'You give me one?'

'Well, well! What do you make of this, Bud?' Chuck called to his friend who had ambled over out of curiosity.

'What's barato?' Bud scratched his head.

'Cheap!' Chuck laughed.

'No cheap!' Pedro cried, emphatically shaking his head.

'El mejor!'

'The best?'

'He's got a cheek!' Bud shook his head in disbelief. 'Reckon all these orphan kids around here are little devils! They'd steal the shirt off your back given half a chance.'

As Chuck looked down indulgently at the little boy, he recognised something familiar in that earnest little face. This could be himself twenty-odd years ago, streetwise from growing up in the slums of the Bronx.

Without hesitation, Chuck glanced quickly around, then went over to the Jeep and came back holding the best watch he had.

'Gracias, Chuck!' Pedro grabbed the watch and ran, clutching it tightly in his hand, ignorant of its real value.

'Are you mad?' Bud said incredulously. 'I don't believe you did that! You could have made hundreds of bucks with that timepiece — and you gave it to a kid!

'You've spent too much time in the sun.' He tapped his head with his finger. 'You're crazy!'

'You don't get it, do you?' Chuck said softly, still watching Pedro's retreating figure with a faraway look in his eyes. 'Doesn't that kid remind you of anyone? Because I'll tell you who he reminds me of — that's us, Bud, you and me twenty years ago!'

There was a pause and then Bud nodded as a slow smile of realisation spread across his face.

'An' I'll tell you something else,' Chuck went on wistfully. 'I like the kid! He's got guts. That little guy will go places!'

Bud slapped Chuck on the back in silent agreement.

* * *

Pedro fumbled awkwardly with the red tissue paper he'd found in the store-room, winding it carefully around the watch, his tongue poking out in concentration.

At the crucial moment, Susanna handed him a bedraggled ribbon which had previously tied back her long hair, and this he wound around the tissue paper parcel before grinning triumphantly.

The end result was far from neat, but Pedro was delighted with it and hurried off to present his gift to his favourite Sister.

Dominique was sitting at a table completing some notes and didn't hear the little boy's approach until he touched her arm.

'Pedro — hello!' She smiled, her pleasure at seeing him turning to pure delight as he handed her the small package. 'What's this — a present, for me?'

Puzzled, she unwrapped it quickly, then gasped when she saw the exquisite watch, nestling in the scrunched-up tissue paper.

'It's beautiful, Pedro! And it's just what I need. How did you know?'

Her heart contracted as she looked at him. He was such a sweet, angelic child — and so thoughtful . . .

Then she looked again at the watch and her smile faded when she saw the make and realised how valuable it was.

Pedro's broad smile began to fade, too.

'But where did you get it, Pedro?' She looked quizzically at the little boy. There was something in his expression, was it guilt — or shame? She couldn't be sure.

'Pedro,' she said quietly, 'You couldn't have bought this. It's obviously very expensive. Does . . . does the watch belong to someone else?

'Tell me the truth now, Pedro,' she continued softly, cupping his chin in her hand and looking a shade reproachfully at him. 'You know I can't accept it if it really belongs to someone else . . .'

There was no mistaking Pedro's expression now. It was shocked and hurt as he backed away from the Sister. As the full meaning of her words began to sink in, he turned and ran, stopping for just a moment to shout back at her.

'I didn't steal it! I didn't . . . but I wish I had — you already think I am a thief anyway!'

Dominique jumped to her feet and made to follow him, but he was too quick.

Tears pricked her eyes when she realised how badly she'd handled the situation. She'd hurt the boy's feelings deeply and she'd give anything to make things right between them.

If Pedro had stolen the watch, and, at the moment, it seemed to be the only explanation, then he had done it with the best possible intentions.

Sighing, she buckled the watch on to her wrist, wondering what to do next.

A few moments later, Chuck entered the hospital tent, carrying a box and found Dominique still staring into space.

'Where do you want these, Sister Dominique?' he called. 'They're those extra bandages you requested.'

'Oh, hello, Chuck,' she said distractedly.

'Could you sign for them?' Chuck pushed a sheet of paper under her nose. 'Hey, that's a good watch you've got there!' He grinned. 'I'll bet that was a surprise for you! That little Pedro — he's something else, ain't' he?

'When he came and asked me for a watch, he made it quite clear he wanted a good one, nothing cheap!'

Dominique looked up. 'You gave Pedro the watch?'

'Sure I did! I couldn't let the kid down when he wanted to surprise his favourite nurse, now could I?'

Dominique felt immediately contrite. She'd misjudged the boy and what was worse, she'd accused him of stealing.

She made up her mind to find Pedro and apologise to him at the first possible opportunity.

* * *

The next day was a tough one at the hospital. Steve Daniels had a long, relentless day in theatre, including a second operation on the young man with the chest wound, and Dominique was assisting him. By the end of the shift, she was exhausted.

She fumbled with the ties on Steve Daniels' operating gown and then stood watching as he pulled it off and tossed it into the laundry bag.

When he sensed her watching him, he turned and grinned.

'I don't know about you, but I could use a walk in the fresh air.'

'Is there anywhere to walk around here?'

'Sure! Come with me and I'll show you!'

Smiling, Dominique tossed her own green gown into the bag and followed Steve Daniels outside. All she had seen of the place so far was muddy, rutted roads and rubble. The forests and mountains, although so close, may well have been a thousand miles away.

They strolled along together, an easy silence between them as they each unwound from the stress of the day.

'Despite all this,' Steve pointed towards the camp, 'it really is a beautiful country.'

Dominique nodded. So far, her chief impression of the place was the humidity — the uncomfortable, sweltering heat which drained all her energy.

'The forest starts just around the next bend.' Steve indicated ahead.

Away from the camp, Dominique had her first taste of the sights and sounds of the forest. It was alive with noise, from stealthy rustles to the loud, screeching calls of the birds.

Even the smell was intoxicating — a mixture of damp vegetation and the heady scent of tropical flowers.

She gazed around her as they walked, for the first time really appreciating the beauty of her surroundings.

The tracks leading into the forest

were short and narrow and it was impossible to venture far before the way became completely blocked by the undergrowth.

'Oh, look!' Suddenly she noticed a tree which had a plant resembling a pineapple growing from a split in the trunk. 'It's a Bromeliad! We keep them as house plants back in England. Oh, I never imagined I'd see anything so lovely growing wild!'

Steve Daniels watched her delight as she appreciated these scents and wonders of the forest.

'You'll never see colour anywhere as vibrant as this,' he said, his enthusiasm infectious. 'Ever seen a humming bird?'

She turned around and shook her head.

'Look,' he pointed. 'Over there . . . see it? It's tiny.'

He put his arms around her shoulders and positioned her so that she could see the bird.

Dominique felt herself tingle involuntarily at his touch.

'What is it?'

'I think it's a tanager,' he whispered. 'It's a songbird. Have you ever seen such amazing colour?'

Dominique looked, fascinated, at the bird with its bright turquoise breast and vibrant green head and wished she had a camera to capture some of the magic before her. Everything was breathtakingly beautiful.

They walked in and out of the forest, marvelling at its luxuriant splendour. Dominique asked many questions and made several interesting observations about the various ferns and flowers growing all around them.

'Have you always been so interested in this sort of thing?' Steve Daniels asked her. 'You seem to be pretty knowledgeable.'

'I enjoy gardening.' She smiled shyly. 'I look after the herb garden at the convent . . . and I grow flowers for the hospital and the chapel. But everything here is so massive! And so brilliant!'

He grinned. 'My interest began at

college when I studied botany, but it's become something of a hobby, even a passion!' His face darkened. 'And it depresses me so much that the rain forests are being destroyed at such a rate,' he said dejectedly.

'I know,' Dominique said sympathetically. 'It saddens me, too. By the time people realise the damage they're doing, it could be too late. We can't afford to lose any more of these amazing places.'

Steve sank his hands into his pockets and heaved his shoulders into a deep sigh.

'You know my dream, Dominique?' Steve turned to her, breaking the silence, his tone lighter now and slightly self-conscious. 'To own a house with a magnificent garden. I'd grow plants from all the places I've been to — a living reminder of the amazing people I've met.'

He looked deep into her eyes and smiled. 'Sounds crazy, doesn't it?'

'No,' Dominique said softly. 'It

doesn't sound crazy at all. I know exactly what you mean.'

Steve surprised himself in finding it so easy to confide in someone he'd known such a short time.

It seemed right somehow. It was as if, instinctively, he'd known that Dominique would understand.

'Well, crazy or not, that's my dream,' he said brightly, his assurance returning. 'I'd like to see it come true one day. I'd honestly like to do it.'

'So would I.' Dominique shivered, but she spoke sincerely. 'So would I.'

★　★　★

At last Dominique tracked down Pedro. He'd been avoiding her, but now he was engrossed with some of the other orphans, playing outside the hospital.

She desperately wanted to apologise to him, to sort things out between them.

'Pedro!' she called and at once the laughter and chattering stopped as the children turned to look at her.

Pedro scrambled to his feet, defiance in his dark eyes as he tossed back his head.

'Pedro, I want to talk to you — please!' Dominique called.

The other children were watching him and for a moment, Dominique held her breath, then with a mocking laugh, Pedro turned and ran away, his friends running behind him.

She was surprised how hurt and disappointed she felt at this rebuff. Pedro was special and now it looked like she'd blown any chance of their being friends again.

Feeling completely wretched, she turned and walked back to the tent she shared with Magda. She was glad it was empty and began to prepare herself for bed.

Then, startled by a sudden scuffling outside the tent, she turned to find Pedro standing in the entrance. He was regarding her still with that air of defiance, but there was something about his manner that allowed Dominique a shred of hope.

He was trying so hard to pretend he didn't care, when it was obvious he did — and it warmed Dominique's heart.

'You wanted to see me?' he said nonchalantly.

'Yes, I did, Pedro.' She invited him to sit beside her. 'I wanted to tell you how very sorry I am. I was wrong to accuse you of stealing the watch — it was very wrong of me and I apologise.'

He shrugged indifferently, but avoided meeting her glance. He had his pride and he was obviously still hurt by Dominique's inference.

'I know I'm asking a lot of you, Pedro,' she went on, her voice shaking slightly, 'but ... but I'd like you to forgive me and for us to be friends again.'

She looked down at the watch and held out her wrist so that Pedro could see she was wearing it.

'It's really lovely, Pedro, and I'll always treasure it. But I treasure your friendship more . . . '

He continued to stare at her, but the defiance was slowly melting.

'You really like it?' he demanded. 'You not just being nice?'

'I really like it.' She smiled, happy that he was at least speaking to her.

'Hokay!' He grinned and at once his face changed from that of a suspicious street kid to that of an angelic child.

'Come here, you scamp!' She held out her arms and pulled him to her in a tight embrace, surprised at how skinny he felt. His black hair was as soft as silk against her cheek as, tenderly, she kissed his head . . .

'Back at last! I'm whacked . . . ' Magda swept into the tent and was aware at once that she'd walked in on something very private.

Pedro tore himself from her arms and fled from the tent, leaving Dominique feeling empty and fulfilled all at the same time, knowing she could easily give a mother's love — yet also knowing that such love was beyond her reach.

'Sorry,' Magda said, her voice soft. 'I wouldn't have barged in like that if I'd realised. You know, you two looked perfect together — like the paintings you see of the Madonna and child,' Magda added dreamily.

Dominique stared disbelievingly at Magda for a moment but, at the same time, she knew she couldn't deny the maternal feelings that had surfaced just now with Pedro.

'We should get ready for bed,' she said, at last, the bright edge to her voice attempting to disguise the sadness she felt.

★   ★   ★

Next morning, Sister Augusta entered the hospital tent, sweeping down the central aisle, her black skirts swishing.

'Have you seen Pedro, Sister Dominique?' she demanded, stopping in front of Dominique as her eyes swept around the peaceful ward. 'No, I don't suppose you have!

'It wouldn't be as quiet as this if he were about!'

'Is he in trouble, Sister Augusta?' Dominique asked fearfully, her instincts to protect and shield him stronger than ever after last night.

'Goodness no!' Sister Augusta actually smiled and Dominique was surprised at how pleasant the older woman looked when she didn't have that stern, forbidding expression on her face. 'On the contrary, I have some good news for the boy!'

Dominique was puzzled as the smiling Sister Augusta laid her hand on the younger nun's arm.

'We've found a home for Pedro! A good home with fine people and I couldn't be more pleased. I'm delighted for him, but, as I say, also for us!

'Think, Sister Dominique, with that little monkey off our hands, our work here will be so much easier!'

Dominique's heart seemed to miss a beat and her mind reeled.

Outwardly, she had to smile and

agree, because that was expected of her, but inside she was devastated.

She loved Pedro with all her heart and she didn't want to lose him!

★ ★ ★

Sister Magda sat on the edge of her bed inside the tent and pulled on her shoes, pausing for a moment to look over at her companion, Sister Dominique.

'You know, this may sound crazy,' she burst out, 'but I can't wait to get to the hospital! I'm really enjoying the work — and the people. They're so spirited and . . . ' She struggled to find the right word.

Dominique smiled understandingly. 'I know what you mean,' she said softly.

Magda stood up and smoothed down her skirts. 'You love it here just as much as I do, don't you?'

Dominique smiled again and nodded to the other nun.

Magda's face was pink and glowing and, for a moment, Dominique almost envied her. Magda knew exactly where she was going in life; she was naturally kind and generous and she wasn't afraid to open her heart to anyone.

But, more importantly, Magda was perfectly content with her life as a nun. She had found her true vocation and, if she had ever suffered doubts, then they were a thing of the past.

Magda looked thoughtful and, momentarily, the rosy bloom seemed to fade from her cheeks.

'Time's flown by since we arrived here and now Sister Augusta's saying that the first of the volunteers may start returning home next week. I don't know about you, but I don't want to go home yet. I want to stay and do whatever I can to help.

'Maybe the immediate emergency is over,' Magda went on, fired again by her irrepressible enthusiasm, 'but I can see there's still so much that needs to be done — long term. These poor, unfortunate people are going to need a lot of help for a long time.

'It's the children that really get to me — and the babies!

'They're so beautiful! It would be wonderful to banish all the unhappiness, poverty and misery from their young lives . . .

'But most of all,' Magda said wistfully, 'I just want them to enjoy being children.'

She looked thoughtful. 'I suppose it's all just a dream but I'd like to do something to help . . . ' Then she straightened up and looked almost shocked at her own outburst.

'Listen to me!' she cried, shaking her head. 'Going on and on to you of all people, who knows exactly what I'm talking about.'

Dominique nodded in agreement. She could appreciate how Magda felt, yet she knew, realistically, there was little any of them could do to improve the situation.

Her own thoughts were with Pedro. A week ago, Sister Augusta had told her that he was going to be adopted by a wealthy family.

He would be well cared for, properly educated and he'd never know what it was to be hungry or alone again. She knew she should be pleased for him, but somehow she couldn't get the sadness out of her soul.

For the first time since Tom had been killed, she had allowed herself to become emotionally involved with another person, and now Pedro, too, was going to be taken from her . . .

She knew it was selfish, to grudge the boy this chance of happiness, but her heart was breaking and she was incapable of being rational.

'But at least we won't have to worry about Pedro,' Magda was saying as if she had read Dominique's mind. 'Sister Augusta says his new parents are kind, and generous, and desperate to have a child of their own.

'They'll be good to him. Being older and having no other children, Pedro will be the centre of their lives. They adore him already, by all accounts.

He'll be in good hands, so try not to worry about him too much, Dominique,' she said.

She glanced at her watch. 'Now, I must get going or I'll be late and I'm holding my very first ante-natal class today! See you later.'

With the exuberant Magda's departure, Dominique was left feeling empty and forlorn.

How could she ever have been so foolish as to allow herself to become so fond of this child when she knew that one day they would have to part?

Sighing, she picked up the breviary which had been given to her by Mother Katherine and turned to her favourite psalm. Normally the words brought her comfort, but today they just blurred before her eyes.

Suddenly the tent flap was pushed roughly aside and Dominique jumped, almost dropping her book on the floor.

Little Pedro was standing just inside the tent, a huge grin on his face, his enormous eyes sparkling with joy. In his arms he clutched his few belongings.

His hair had been slicked back and neatly combed and he was wearing new clothes which he drew attention to at once.

'Pretty cool, huh?' he said, adopting a pseudo-American accent.

'You look really smart, Pedro,' Dominique said warmly.

The dark-eyed, olive-skinned little boy sat down on Magda's bed, scuffing his feet on the floor as he talked.

'I'm going to live in a big house, Sister. Really big! I'm going to have my own room — all to myself. And toys and books. And more new clothes . . . and a school uniform for my new school!' His voice rose in excitement.

Dominique felt a wave of anxiety wash over her. A new life, a new school . . . It would be such a huge change. How would Pedro fit in? She hoped the other children would be kind to him.

'You must be sure and go to school, Pedro,' she said softly, remembering tales of his erratic attendance at the mission school.

He usually went barefoot, which was probably why he was waving his feet about for Dominique to admire his shoes; and probably, Dominique thought, why he didn't look quite himself. The Pedro she knew was usually grubby, his hair black and unruly.

' . . . and there's a swimming pool in the garden . . . ' Pedro was becoming breathless, he had so much to say.

'Oh, Pedro! When did you tear your shirt? Your new parents will be here for you any minute.'

Her gaze then went from the tear in the sleeve of his shirt to the knees of his trousers. They were all grubby and his smart leather shoes were scuffed.

He fingered the tear and bit his lip.

'Take it off,' Dominique was searching for her small sewing kit. 'I'll mend it for you.'

'I fell off my skateboard!' He looked away sheepishly. 'Loads of times!'

'You've been skateboarding in your

new clothes?' Dominique laughed. 'You rascal!'

'They bought it for me, Luis and Dorotea, when they took me shopping. They let me choose any toy I wanted!'

She looked up from her sewing. 'I want you to promise you'll be a good boy for Luis and Dorotea,' she said. 'Work hard at school and they'll be proud of you. And I'll be proud, too, Pedro.'

'I'll try, Sister!' He grinned impishly.

'Where is the skateboard, by the way?' Dominique asked.

Pedro looked worriedly down at his feet, the way he always looked when he'd done something wrong or naughty.

'Oh, Pedro, you haven't broken it already?'

'No, nothing like that. I gave it to Jose and the other boys. Do you think Luis and Dorotea will mind? I wanted to give my friends something and . . . and it was all I had.'

'Oh, Pedro, they won't mind a bit!' Again Dominique was touched by the little orphan's thoughtfulness.

She snipped the cotton and passed him his shirt. 'And be more careful!' She pretended to admonish him and then she straightened his collar and smoothed down his hair. Then she took a cloth and rubbed it over his shoes.

Finally, she brushed his trousers while he stood still, watching her and enjoying being fussed over.

'There, that's better. You'll do now!' Then she packed his things carefully into a carrier bag and, with a falsely bright smile, handed it to him. 'Take care, Pedro — and don't forget me, will you?'

'I won't, Sister Dominique. And I'll make you proud of me!'

He looked at her so earnestly that her heart fluttered. There was no denying the special bond between them. It hadn't all been one-sided.

'Your watch — ' he asked almost shyly ' — is she still working well?'

'Yes, yes it is, Pedro,' she replied softly. 'It's going beautifully. I'll always treasure it . . . every time I look at the time, I'll think of my Pedro.'

He stared at her with his soft, dark eyes.

She fell silent, then slowly she removed her rosary, holding it in her hands and looking hard at it for a long moment before handing it to him.

'I want you to have this, Pedro. A present from me.'

He gazed up at her in disbelief. He had admired the rosary from the very first time he'd seen it. He'd wanted to touch the intricate crucifix, had even 'borrowed' it for a little while . . . now she was giving it to him . . .

'Sometimes, perhaps, you'll look at it and think of me and remember what good friends we were.'

'I'll never forget you, Sister Dominique! Never!' Pedro said vehemently, holding the rosary tightly against his chest. 'I promise.'

6

'Ah, there you are.' A nurse looked into the tent. 'Come along, Pedro, your new family has arrived. You can say goodbye to this place for ever!' she added cheerfully.

Dominique, realising that the moment she had been dreading had come, embraced Pedro tightly and he returned her hug just as fiercely.

'Come on,' she said, forcing a smile and taking hold of his hand. 'We mustn't keep Luis and Dorotea waiting.'

Outside, the sun seemed particularly hot and brilliant as they made their way over to where a well-dressed couple were waiting beside their car.

Dorotea was a small, pretty woman with long, dark hair glimmering with silver streaks, and a warm smile which lit up her eyes.

Her husband, Luis, was tall and dark, and he had friendly, brown eyes.

Dominique was sure they would lavish love and care on Pedro and that he would be happy with them.

'Be happy, Pedro,' she said gently, giving him a little push towards them. 'God bless you.'

Then the dark-eyed little boy who'd won her heart walked towards his new family, stopping once to look back. The love in his eyes was so intense that it made Dominique's stomach tighten. But she smiled encouragingly at him, willing him to keep going.

They hugged him in welcome, drawing him into their secure world.

She stood with the others, waving as the car bounced away down the uneven road until it was out of sight. Dominique's last image was of Pedro, his face a blur, his hand raised in a final wave.

Someone standing close to Dominique was laughing.

'What a character! We're going to

miss having young Pedro around.'

It was Chuck Weisman talking to one of the nurses.

Dominique couldn't keep up the pretence a moment longer. Pedro had gone from her life for ever and she was going to miss him dreadfully.

Walking stiffly, she quickly made for the nearest tent, barely getting out of sight before breaking down.

She covered her face with her hands, giving way at last to the utter misery she felt inside. She slumped to the ground as uncontrollable sobs racked her body.

* * *

Dr Steve Daniels saw Sister Dominique heading for the supply tent and followed her, hoping to discuss the coming day's schedules with her.

Then he heard her muffled sobs coming from the far corner of the tent. He stopped in his tracks, stunned by the intensity of her grief. He'd known she was fond of the little boy, but hadn't realised how deep her feelings went.

He wished there was something he could do to comfort her, but felt instinctively that she needed to be alone and wouldn't welcome an intrusion. He drew back into the shadows, reluctant to leave her entirely alone.

That afternoon, when Father Gomez came to the hospital to visit the injured, Dominique sought him out to ask after Esteban, the young man who'd lost his wife in the disaster.

'I'm glad you asked, Sister,' he said and, taking her by the elbow, guided Dominique away from the rows of beds. 'I wanted to have a word with you about that young man ... I really thought you'd got through to him ... it's so disappointing ... '

'I take it there has been no real change in his attitude then?' Dominique said sadly.

'I'm afraid not.' Father Gomez shook his head gravely. 'I just don't know what to do for the best. He's completely unreasonable. He won't listen to me at all . . . I was hoping you'd speak to him again, Sister Dominique . . . '

'Of course, Father, if you think it will help.'

'The fact is, he's getting worse, Sister.' Father Gomez looked and sounded extremely concerned. 'He's been getting into fights; he barely eats or sleeps and he's rude and offensive to everyone who tries to help him.

'The thing is he isn't a bad man, Sister. Before all this, he was a good, honest young man who wouldn't harm a fly. Now he's drunk most of the time and brawling in the streets. His friends have all deserted him and there doesn't seem to be any way to get through to him.'

Suddenly Father Gomez looked worried. 'Perhaps it's not such a good idea for you to speak to him . . . '

Dominique gave a short laugh. 'Father, I haven't always been a nun, remember, just as you haven't always been a priest. I'm not easily shocked if that's what's worrying you! I'll try talking to him again.'

★   ★   ★

Now that she was standing outside the ruined house which had once been home to Esteban and his young bride, Rosamunda, Dominique had an overwhelming desire to turn on her heel and run.

But she forced herself to pick her way through the rubble, calling Esteban's name and searching for some sign of him.

She peered through the broken window into the dim interior. Empty bottles and cans were strewn across the floor, but the place seemed abandoned now.

She went back on to the street, looking up and down.

'You looking for me, Sister?'

She spun round. Esteban had come from the direction of the house she had presumed deserted. He was standing in what was left of the doorway, swaying slightly.

His black hair was dirty and his skin looked sallow and unhealthy. He was covered in bruises from fights and the stubble on his chin had grown into an untidy beard. He had sunk into total lethargy.

'Hello, Esteban,' she said softly in fluent Spanish. 'I'm Sister Dominique. Remember? Yes, I am looking for you. Could we talk?'

She felt a surge of compassion for him. He looked so lost and bewildered standing there and she knew he must have loved Rosamunda very much to have reached such a low ebb.

'I know you.' He held up a can of beer and pointed it at her. 'You were at the Father's place . . . tried to tell me that your God loves me,' he sneered.

'He's your God, too,' she whispered.

Her heart was hammering. His eyes looked so dark and hostile.

'I've come to talk to you, Esteban,'

she said softly. 'To help you. I know how you feel . . . '

He turned away abruptly, and went back into the wreckage of his home.

Dominique followed him, anxious to take a closer look at a deep cut close to his eye.

'Let me look at that cut, Esteban,' she pleaded, reaching up. 'It needs attention . . . '

He flinched away.

'Get to the point, Sister,' Esteban snapped, then turned his back on her again as if he had already given her all the time he was prepared to spare for talking.

'You can't go on living like this, Esteban,' she began. 'You must begin to rebuild your life . . . and your home.'

He swung round to face her, eyes flashing.

'There's no point. Not without my Rosamunda!' He slammed his fist into the wall in despair.

Dominique spoke nervously. 'Please, believe me, Esteban. You don't have to go through this alone. People want to help you,' she pleaded. 'I want to tell you about my experience — God does love you.'

'What would you know?' He spun round, eyes flashing angrily, his cheeks fiery red. 'You — a nun! Safe and secure in your self-righteous little world. Cut off from life's misery and pain!'

Dominique smarted at his unjust taunts. How could he say such things when she was surrounded by suffering?

His own pain was making him speak irrationally.

His eyes were blazing with fury, but Dominique stood her ground, determined not to be put off. There had to be a way to reach this grief-stricken man.

'Esteban, I . . . ' she began.

Again he interrupted her savagely. 'You don't know what it is to love someone, let alone lose them before you've even had a life together . . .

'Why don't you just go back where

you belong, to your prayers and your safe, remote existence — and just leave me alone!'

But Dominique persisted.

'I do understand.'

'You don't! You know nothing of life — of real life! So what right do you have to preach to me?' he yelled.

Dominique clenched her teeth. She was becoming angry with this man. He was wallowing in his own grief.

She had seen so much pain and suffering since she arrived here, and had nothing but admiration for the way most people had coped with loss and grief.

'Do you really think you're the only person who's ever lost someone they loved?' Her voice was low to start with, scarcely audible but she became more agitated as anger bubbled inside her.

'I find your attitude incredible, Esteban. I honestly think you believe you're the first person ever to suffer this agony! Well, you're wrong, Esteban, very wrong!'

He made to sneer, but the furiously dark look on her face stunned him into silence.

She could feel the rage surging through her as she spoke.

'I lost my own husband just after we were married. I watched them carry his dead body down from the mountain where he had died.'

Her voice shook, but there was no self-pity, only acceptance.

'Yes, Esteban, I had to accept that the man I loved and respected with all my heart was gone — for ever.

'He was my whole life. I lived only for him. Then today I had to say goodbye to someone else I'd grown to care for deeply.

'But I get on with my life. I make the best of things . . . and it's not easy. Look out there.' She grabbed him by his shirt and pulled him over to the broken window.

'What makes you think you're the only one? Haven't you eyes to see the misery and suffering that surrounds you?

'Look . . . over the road, there. Those people lost their four children in the earthquake, but are they wallowing in self-pity? Well, are they?' she repeated angrily.

'No, Esteban — they're out there rebuilding their home, trying to make the best of things, despite their grief.

'You should come up to the hospital some time. See the children and babies we have there, all of them orphans; children who've lost limbs, who are learning to live with a handicap. What chance do you suppose they have of rebuilding their lives in this place?

'Not much, if we're completely honest with ourselves. Yet they're not giving in.'

She turned away, leaving him staring out at the street. She was shaking with emotion and she could see that he was, too.

But she was too angry to relent now. Angry for losing Tom, for losing Pedro. Angry for all the victims of this terrible earthquake.

'I'll tell you, Esteban. If your wife could see you now . . . ' He turned to look at her. 'If Rosamunda could see you now, she would be ashamed!

'By all accounts, you're not the man she married . . .

'All you've done is hurt people, especially Father Gomez. Go on . . . ' She picked up a can of beer from the table and shoved it into his hands. 'Drink yourself to death!

'You've gone beyond help. Even God can't help you if you've turned against Him!

'I wash my hands of you!' she said scornfully. 'And if Father Gomez has any sense, he'll stop wasting his time on you and help those who really need it!'

She stared at him, wide-eyed, openly letting him see her contempt before turning on her heel and taking her leave.

★ ★ ★

Chuck looked across the table at his companion, Elena. She was beautiful, her untamed black curls fanned across her narrow shoulders and curled about her small, dark face.

This girl he'd rescued from the rubble was always happy, always laughing and Chuck knew he was the envy of all the other guys tonight.

She was laughing at him now, her sparkling white teeth gleaming like the whites of her captivating dark brown eyes.

'Sure you don't want to dance any more, Chuck?' She pouted.

'Maybe later, Elena.' He grinned. He'd been flattered by all the attention she paid him and he'd hardly been able to take his eyes off her.

Now he was feeling light-headed from having drunk more than he normally would and her eyes, those wonderful eyes, were somehow hypnotic.

For some inexplicable reason, being with Elena made him feel as if home wasn't so very far away.

'OK.' Elena finished her drink and put her glass down. 'I got a better idea, Chuck. We buy some wine and we take it back to my place?'

She was looking at him again, directly challenging him. His mouth felt dry. The temptation was more than he could bear. Getting up, he grinned at her and went over to the bar.

She stood beside him, clinging to his arm and gazing up at him enticingly.

As he put his arm around her, Elena's heady perfume filled his senses and he was finding it hard to breathe.

As he fumbled for some notes, Chuck almost dropped his wallet. He saw something flutter to the floor and, when he bent down to pick it up, realised it was a snapshot of his wife and their baby.

Shelley was laughing out at him, her pretty face framed by short, blonde hair. In her arms, baby Joe grinned, too. He had his mother's blue eyes and his father's dark hair.

Chuck had never cheated on Shelley, never.

'That your kid?' Elena took the photograph and looked at it for a moment. 'He's gonna be a real heartbreaker, just like his dad.'

She carefully made no mention of his wife.

Chuck took the photograph back and tucked it safely in his wallet. If he went home with Elena tonight, he'd never forgive himself. He couldn't betray Shelley, no matter how lonely he felt.

'Come on, Chuck. Let's go.' Elena was impatient.

'Sorry, babe.' He kissed her lightly on the forehead. 'I've got to be getting back to camp — I'm on early tomorrow.'

'Oh, Chuck! What about our . . . date?' she asked provocatively.

'Sorry, honey,' he mumbled and turned away. 'See you around.'

Elena watched him leave and sighed sadly. He was a nice guy who'd do anything for anyone, and he was too much in love with his wife to look for love elsewhere.

As Chuck reached the door, he noticed a lone figure at one of the tables, standing up as he passed. As the man came out of the shadows, he realised it was Father Gomez and the priest was smiling warmly.

'Well done, Chuck. You did the right thing. I'm proud of you. There aren't many men who could say no to Elena.'

'Then how come it hurts so much, Father?' Chuck said gloomily.

'If you had gone home with Elena, you would have hurt more, tomorrow . . . and for the rest of your life.'

Father Gomez patted his shoulder and together they walked out of the taverna.

Outside, they paused to look up at the stars which covered the cloudless sky.

'It's not always easy to do the right think, Chuck. After all, we're only human,' he said quietly. 'Are you going back to camp?'

'There's nowhere else for me to go, Father,' Chuck said ruefully.

'I'll walk along with you,' Father Gomez said cheerfully.

'Thanks, Father.' Chuck smiled. 'I could sure use some company.'

7

The peace of the forest was shattered as birds shrieked and crashed through the trees in a cacophony of noise.

Steve Daniels was sitting on a fallen tree, looking down at the waterfall cascading over the rocks below. He hardly heard the sounds coming from the depths of the forest — his mind was absorbed with something else.

'Ow!'

He looked up sharply as Lisa Wayne slapped her leg.

'Something bit me!' she cried. 'Damn bugs! It beats me what you like about this place.' She shuddered. 'It's beautiful, but . . . it gives me the creeps.'

He looked up at her. She was standing up, running her hands through her hair which clung damply around her face. She was a lovely girl and he cared a lot for her, but finding the right words to tell her that he didn't love her enough to marry her was proving more difficult than he'd ever imagined.

The last time he'd had time to come here was when Sister Dominique accompanied him. He'd recalled the wonder and enchantment in her eyes and the excitement in her voice as she made discovery after discovery in the rain forest.

If only he could feel as relaxed now as he did that day. But he was on edge, dreading saying what had to be said.

'Lisa . . . '

'Time we got back to camp,' she said, glancing at him. Then, puzzled at his solemn expression, she asked, 'What's wrong, Steve?'

'Sit down for a minute, Lisa, will you?' he said carefully. 'I want to talk to you.'

'So that's why you brought me all this way? You spend the past week avoiding me, then out of the blue you ask me to come for a walk — sounds

115

ominous!' She laughed. 'What have I done, Steve? Better tell me and get it over with.'

'It's nothing you've done, Lisa,' he said, looking into her eyes, hoping she'd understand. 'It's me, I . . . '

Lisa paled and her lovely eyes seemed to grow enormous in her face. His unhappy expression troubled her.

'It's — it's just, well, I think the world of you, Lisa, you know that. But I . . . I just don't love you. So our future . . . '

Dismayed, she looked away as tears misted her eyes. She felt humiliated. She would have done anything for this man and she'd thought he felt the same way about her.

'It wouldn't work out, Lisa,' he went on quickly. 'There just isn't that spark between us.' His voice faltered. 'But I want us to stay friends.'

She looked sharply at him.

'Friends?' she whispered as tears splashed on to her cheeks. 'Is that all I am to you?'

'I wouldn't have hurt you like this for the world, but . . . '

Lisa tried to smile. 'No . . . no, I'm glad you've been honest.' She sniffed, taking out her handkerchief, rubbing her eyes, then taking a deep breath to steady herself. 'I've been so naïve, Steve, assuming that we were going to . . . '

She looked up at the sky and sighed. Then she got up and brushed at her trousers.

'We'd better be getting back,' she said. 'Would you know I've been crying?'

Her eyes were red, but Steve shook his head.

'You look great,' he said softly. 'Lisa, I'm so sorry . . . '

'I — I can't go on working with you, Steve. It would be just impossible now. I'm going to see Sister Augusta as soon as we get back.

'I'll arrange to get away from here as soon as possible. I want to go home, back to the States.'

It was two days before Dominique managed to speak to Father Gomez. She'd been to his tent several times, but Maria, his housekeeper, was always full of apologies, saying that the Father was out.

This time, however, she was lucky to find him there.

Dominique stepped into the cool interior of the tent. Father Gomez looked up at her from his seat at the table and smiled benignly.

'Hello, Sister Dominique. What can I do for you?' His smile faded when he saw how troubled she looked, worse than the day she had first told him of her doubts.

'I have to talk to you, Father,' she said unhappily.

'That's what I'm here for, child.' He got up and pulled a chair from under the table.

'It's about Esteban,' she said as she sat down. 'I went to see him and . . .

and . . . Oh, Father, I've made such a terrible mess of things.

'I lost my temper with him and said some cruel, unforgivable things. Instead of bringing him hope and comfort, I told him he was weak! I more or less called him a fool!'

Father Gomez nodded, smiling indulgently, waiting for Dominique to continue.

'I said . . . ' She bit her lip. 'Oh Father, I told him that Rosamunda would be ashamed of him and that God wouldn't help him because he'd turned his back on his faith . . . '

'Is that all?' Father Gomez enquired softly of her then.

'I wish it were.' She looked down at her hands. 'I told him he might as well drink himself to death!' She looked aghast at the priest. 'Can you imagine?

'If anything happens to Esteban, if he does anything stupid, I'll never forgive myself . . . '

'Have you finished?' Father Gomez asked and Dominique nodded.

'Then I have something to tell you, Sister. Esteban came to see me today. He appeared here first thing this morning.

'He was clean-shaven and sober.' The priest beamed, unable to contain his joy.

'His struggle is far from over, but he's started on the road to recovery. He was quiet and subdued and, when I asked him what had brought about his change of heart, he told me quite simply that it was all down to a raving firebrand of a nun!'

Dominique gasped and Father Gomez laughed heartily.

'He also told me that this nun was the first person he'd spoken to who seemed to understand what he was going through.'

Father Gomez smiled fondly.

'What — what else did he say?' Dominique asked hesitantly.

'He's determined to make a real effort to piece his life back together again and he's promised to stop blaming everyone else for his misfortunes. Most importantly, he's stopped blaming God.

'And do you see how God is helping you, Sister Dominique? In His own way, He's showing you what to do. You reached Esteban where I had failed.'

Dominique nodded, relief flooding through her and she felt her anger with herself subsiding.

'I've been so worried about Esteban,' she confessed. 'You don't know how glad I am that he's all right.'

'I think I do, Sister . . . ' Father Gomez reached across the table and took her hand. 'I think I understand something else, too.

'Maybe, in bringing you here, God is trying to show you what is right for you . . . showing you your way ahead.'

Dominique looked steadily at the priest, her heart beginning to pound. If only he were right . . . for she knew the way ahead for her was still far from clear.

★ ★ ★

'Sister! Sister!'

Sister Dominique looked up, suddenly realising that the whole of the operating staff were staring at her. Over the top of his mask, Dr Steve Daniels' blue eyes blazed. Dominique felt momentarily confused. For an instant she had let her mind drift from the job in hand — and that was unforgivable.

'Sorry,' she mumbled, her cheeks burning beneath her mask. 'I . . . '

Steve Daniels sighed impatiently. It wasn't the first time he'd had to speak sharply to Sister Dominique, yet still she seemed unable to stop her mind from wandering. Her concentration was not all it should be.

'This may be a routine operation, Sister, but I'd appreciate your co-operation here!' he said shortly. 'Be ready with a clamp, will you?'

For a moment there was an awkward silence, then she nodded, glancing around nervously as everyone settled back to work.

She knew she hadn't been concentrating — she'd been thinking about Pedro. Was he happy? Was he managing to settle down all right with his new parents?

And yet Pedro was only a part of the tangled thoughts and feelings churning around inside her. She missed him terribly, and it was bringing home to her exactly what her life was lacking.

Her eyes misted and she quickly blinked back tears, trying hard to concentrate.

Suddenly she became aware again of Steve Daniels' voice. Clearly he was waiting for her to pass him something.

Flustered and embarrassed, Dominique turned and fumbled through the instruments on the trolley, until she found what she thought Steve had asked for. But as she passed it to him, it dropped from her hands and clattered to the floor.

Once again all eyes seemed to turn on her. Her own eyes widened as she glanced nervously at Steve.

The young doctor was glaring at her angrily.

'I . . . I . . . ' She tried to stammer out an apology, but her throat had gone dry.

'Nurse Harris.' The doctor turned to the junior nurse. 'Perhaps you could pass me the sutures.'

Dominique looked at the scissors lying on the floor in bewilderment. Sutures? She could have sworn he asked for scissors.

And now as she watched Steve at work, cool and precise, she found, to her horror, that she couldn't recall a single moment of the operation.

Behind her mask, she bit hard on her lips.

Then, suddenly, it was all over. Steve Daniels strode abruptly away from the operating table and, for the first time since she'd been working with him, Dominique realised he hadn't taken the time to thank his team before leaving.

'I'll go and help him disrobe,' Nurse Harris said quickly. 'Can you manage to finish off in here?'

Dominique nodded.

In the curtained-off ante-room, Steve Daniels scrubbed furiously at his hands and arms. Nurse Harris approached him warily, but he clearly wanted no help at all from her.

His mask dangling loosely around his neck, he swung round, his expression grim.

'Nurse! Tell Sister Dominique I want to see her as soon as she's scrubbed up,' he barked and the junior nurse flinched at his unaccustomed brusqueness.

'In my office!' he added.

'I wouldn't like to be in Sister Dominique's shoes when Dr Daniels is finished with her!' A passing orderly shook his head sympathetically.

At that moment, the curtain moved aside and Dominique came into the ante-room, and walked over to the wash basin. She looked tired and weary, but mustered a smile for the orderly and Nurse Harris.

They exchanged looks, wondering if she had overheard them talking about her. Both could see she was deeply troubled about something.

Dominique was vexed at herself and she understood Steve's annoyance. She would have felt the same way in the past when she had responsibility.

'Sister.' Nurse Harris cleared her throat. 'Dr Daniels wants to see you . . . right away.'

'Thank you,' she said quietly, carefully folding her gown and placing it neatly in the laundry bag. Then, bracing herself, she stepped out of the anteroom and walked the short distance to the doctor's office.

She paused outside, taking a couple of deep breaths to try to calm herself. After that nightmare in theatre, she was convinced she was about to be relieved of her position.

* * *

Steve Daniels sat at his desk, head bowed over the paperwork which had to be completed after every operation. A desk lamp cast a dim glow around the room.

It was only when Dominique reached the desk that she realised he wasn't working. He glanced up as she approached, and she looked quickly away, afraid to meet his eyes.

'Sit down, Sister.' He gestured to a chair and it was impossible to gauge his mood from the tone of his voice.

Obediently, she sat down, staring down at her hands. When she looked up at him, she thought she saw his expression soften.

'What's wrong, Dominique?' he asked, his voice soft and genuinely concerned. 'You're just not yourself today. I've never known you perform badly in theatre before, but, just now . . .

'An outsider could have been forgiven for thinking that it was your first operation! Something must be badly wrong for you to be in this state.' The last was said with a measure of exasperation.

Dominique considered for a moment, before replying tersely.

'I think that's my business, don't you?'

She lowered her head again, her face in shadow, but Steve Daniels could still see the glint of tears in her eyes.

'Not when it's affecting my patients! Then it's very much my business!' His voice rose and she looked up at him in desperation.

She knew she owed him an explanation, but somehow the words wouldn't come.

He saw her despair, but had the feeling if he pressed her a little harder she might open up to him and talk.

'The day Pedro left,' he began gently, coaxing, 'you looked very upset so I followed you into the tent . . . '

Her eyes widened in surprise.

'I didn't mean to intrude,' he went on and now his voice was kind, under-standing. 'I really wanted to talk to you, but when I realised you were crying . . . I sensed you needed to be alone.'

She stiffened for a moment, then realised that if she didn't talk to someone soon about how she felt, someone outside the church, she would be driven mad by the turmoil raging inside her.

He watched her carefully, waiting patiently for her to open up. She was everything a nun should be in her words and manner, but he had never seen one look so haunted — and he had worked with many all over the world during his time as a relief surgeon.

The concern in his eyes was too much for Dominique. She couldn't keep her feelings bottled up any longer.

'When I left England,' she began, 'I was already beginning to doubt my vocation . . . it was nothing I could explain, nothing I could put my finger on, just a general sense of uncertainty.

'It was hoped that coming here would help me find my way.' She smiled mirthlessly. 'But all it's done is make matters worse.

'I feel as though I'm on the brink of making a vital decision in my life, but my feelings are so confused, I don't know which way that decision will take me.'

'Being here is enough to confuse anyone,' Steve Daniels murmured. 'It's far from a normal situation.

'Perhaps it isn't the right place for you to find whatever it is you're looking for.'

She was glad of the dim light. It helped mask the sadness in her eyes. She could sense he was no longer angry; but it was as well she couldn't see the compassion on his face or she might have broken down completely.

'After . . . after Tom, my husband, died, I thought that being a nun was enough. I was content, fulfilled . . . but lately, more and more, my doubts have been increasing.'

She broke off, embarrassed, aware that a nun was not supposed to feel like this, let alone admit to an outsider that she harboured such feelings. But it was too late to stop.

'And I think it was little Pedro who finally brought out my true feelings,' she went on, her heart contracting at the very thought of the little boy who had stolen her heart.

'He puts on this street-wise, tough guy front, yet he's so vulnerable. He needs a mother's love,' she said huskily. 'I found myself growing to love him so quickly, so easily . . . until I was almost thinking of him as my own child.

'Do you realise what that means?' She looked appealingly at him. 'It means,' she went on, without waiting for his reply, 'that I've been tearing myself apart ever since he left.

'Not only because I miss him so much, but because I've suddenly become aware that I'm not just a nurse, not just a nun. I'm a woman with all a woman's needs. I can't ignore them any more but, at the same time, I don't know how to handle the feelings.'

'I think I can understand,' he said softly. 'But, Dominique, surely you know better than to allow yourself to become involved emotionally under the circumstances.

'You're a nurse as well as a nun and I know that compassion plays a large rôle in your life, your work, but with so many people needing help, why single out Pedro as a special case?'

She shrugged hopelessly. 'I don't know — it's just being with Pedro and doing all the special little things I did with him . . . ' She gave a wry smile. 'Well, that brought everything home to me, I suppose. My time with Pedro — it's the nearest I'll ever come to being a mother myself.'

Steve was taken aback by her frank admission. 'But, Dominique, surely you knew that there'd be little chance of motherhood when you took your vows?'

He looked pensive. 'On the other hand,' he said slowly, 'I think I know you well enough to say that you wouldn't have made them lightly . . . '

'I know,' she said brokenly, 'I know. It's just that I feel differently now. I can't help it.'

She sounded utterly desolate, and Steve longed to comfort her, to put an arm round her.

But this was no ordinary woman, he reminded himself and he was all too aware of the need to tread carefully.

Steve stood up, walked around the desk and leaned on it, right in front of Dominique.

She looked up at him, but his face was swathed in shadows and it was impossible to see his expression.

'I guess I never really thought about — how much a woman has to give up to pursue her career — or her vocation — before. I'm sorry, Dominique.'

Impulsively, he reached out and gently squeezed her shoulder. Then, withdrawing his hand quickly, Steve got up and returned to his chair.

He smiled at her across the desk, a smile tinged with sadness.

'Whatever else,' he said sincerely,

'you're an exceptionally good nurse, Dominique, and it's pretty clear to me that you just weren't feeling yourself today. We all have our off days.'

'I'm really sorry about that,' she said, beginning to feel better. 'I promise it won't happen again. Thank you for letting me explain . . . and for . . . for being so understanding.'

She got up and he watched her leave, deep in thought. He had always held a high opinion of her as a nurse and nothing had changed that.

He still respected her and wanted her on his team, but Sister Dominique was clearly very vulnerable and confused.

With a deep sigh, he picked up a pen and bowed his head over the paperwork on his desk.

Now that the state of emergency was over, heavy earth-moving equipment had cleared most of the rubble away in preparation for the massive rebuilding operation. But all this left Sister Magda feeling troubled — enough to confide her worries to the local priest.

'But, Sister Magda — ' Father Gomez was a little puzzled by the young nun's fears. 'Why feel guilty, when your intentions are so good?'

'Because for the first time in my life, I want to go against God's will,' she explained.

Now it was Father Gomez's turn to feel confused. 'What exactly is it that you want to do, Sister?'

'I want to stay here, Father!' she blurted out hurriedly.

Father Gomez was not entirely surprised. He'd noticed the bloom in her cheeks as she worked with the local people, seen the love shine in her eyes for them.

'I know I should be following the path that God has chosen for me, Father,' she went on. 'And I feel so guilty when there are people, the world over, who need help and spiritual guidance. Oh, Father,' she said dispiritedly, 'what am I to do? I feel so selfish.'

For a moment the priest considered. Sister Magda never failed to impress him with her tireless effort. She was a first-class nun, devoted to her vocation.

Never once had he heard her utter an impatient word, even when her patience must have been sorely tried by those she was tying to help. But answering her cry for help wasn't going to be easy although he understood precisely how she felt.

Finally he said, 'You should never feel guilty about wanting to do good.

'Remember, too, Sister, that everyone's faith is tested at some time or other, but I truly believe that wherever God leads you, it will be to do His work.'

Magda nodded, relieved. She felt better for unburdening herself of her worries, but still, deep down, was the niggling feeling that leaving this place and the people she had grown to love would be the hardest thing she had ever been asked to do in her life.

As she left the wooden-framed tent to be met outside by the humid heat of the day, she couldn't help remembering her first impression of Father Gomez, slumped over a table, undeniably drunk!

Smiling wryly to herself, she vowed never to pre-judge anyone so harshly again.

★　★　★

Dominique made her way through piled-up boxes, kitbags and other paraphernalia which was in the process of being moved out of the camp.

She stopped for a moment and looked around. The GIs were all busy, loading their equipment on to trucks and Jeeps ready for their imminent departure. Only a few key personnel were staying on now that the worst of the emergency was over. She moved on, dust drying her lips and throat, searching for one familiar face in particular.

'Chuck!' she cried when she saw him, standing beside his Jeep, a cigarette dangling from the side of his mouth.

When he saw her, he grinned, tossed

the cigarette down and stamped it out with his boot.

Ever since she had learned that the American soldiers were moving out, she'd been desperate to find him, to say goodbye. He had been the first person she'd met and had brought a welcome levity to her sometimes troubled stay.

And, like her, he had become close to Pedro, too.

'Chuck.' She gave in to the urge to hug him. 'Things just aren't going to be the same around here without you!'

'Oh, gee! You'll manage, Sister.' He grinned bashfully.

'There are so many things I should thank you for . . . ' she began ' . . . like looking out for Pedro, for instance! And giving him this lovely watch so that he could give it to me . . . that was really generous . . . I appreciate it.'

'You deserve it,' Chuck declared firmly. 'There were plenty of ways you helped me, too, Sister.'

He paused for a moment, then cleared his throat.

'I've been all over the world and I guess I've seen a lot of hardship and pain, but here, in the face of tragedy, I've — well, I've seen courage . . . and strength, and kindness.'

'I think we've all had our eyes opened, Chuck,' Dominique said soberly.

'It goes deeper than that.' Chuck patted his chest. 'Just watching you and the Sisters and seeing your great faith and determination has, well, sort of rubbed off on me . . .

'I remember seeing your face when you first came here, when you realised the child in your arms was dead. I thought you'd never stay the course, but you have and you've done us all proud.

'I feel like I've 'grown' from my time here and for having known you, Sister. I'm a stronger person,' he added, diffidently shrugging his wide, bony shoulders as if such sentimental words were hard for him to say.

'Being here — ' He looked around the camp with its domed and wooden-framed tents, and rough wooden huts.

'Being here has taught me to count my blessings.'

They stood for a moment, smiling shyly, both unwilling to say goodbye first. At last Chuck held out his hand and took Dominique's in a firm grip.

'Goodbye, Sister. Take care of yourself. I won't forget you.'

'Nor me, Chuck.' She released his hand and watched as he jumped into his Jeep. 'God bless you and your family . . . 'bye. Take care.'

She watched as his Jeep joined the rest of the convoy, and vanished into a cloud of dust. His parting words kept going round and round in her mind.

He felt a better person for being here, stronger, that's what he'd said. She waited until the Jeep was out of sight, then turned back into the camp.

If only she felt stronger she thought gloomily. All being here had done for her was to weaken her calling still further and cast even more doubts in her path.

8

The hospital tent was quiet now, with only a few patients remaining and Dominique found, for the first time since her arrival, that she had time on her hands.

It was the same in the evening. Having finished off some odd jobs and small chores at the hospital for the day, she attended the service in the make-shift chapel. Afterwards Dominique found herself with nothing to occupy her except her own turbulent thoughts. Thoughts she would rather be without. It almost seemed as if she never had time to think about anything else. Absently she ran her fingers through her long dark hair and sighed deeply.

It was too early for bed. She poked her head outside and breathed in the evening air. It was never anything else but warm but tonight a cooling, pleasant breeze had wafted in from somewhere, blowing away the usual uncomfortable humidity, at least for a time.

Far too perfect an evening to waste. And she didn't know how much longer she'd be in this place — she realised she could be sent home at any time now that the immediate danger was over.

Without the GIs, the camp seemed deadly quiet as she made her way through the tents towards the path which led to the edge of the forest.

Remembering Steve Daniels' warning to be careful, she followed the path into the forest which she knew was not too overgrown.

It was refreshingly cool amongst the lush, dense undergrowth and she walked slowly, savouring the incredibly beautiful sights and sounds all around her.

Occasionally she lingered to watch a bird or to gaze at a flower. The colours amazed her, dazzling, shimmering, vibrant colours. And things seemed so huge that she felt like a shrunken Alice in Wonderland, wandering through a giant garden.

Trees towered above her, so tall that if she looked to their tops, her head would spin.

Before her the path forked. She looked along the familiar route, then to the newer one. It was quite overgrown, but passable with care, and she felt the urge to explore.

The new path was steep and twisting in places and she slid and slithered, grasping at vines to stay on her feet.

All at once, she found herself in a clearing. Before her, a fast-moving stream flowed into a rushing waterfall at the end of the other path.

Here, the birds squealed and squawked in a deafening chorus, heralding the coming of darkness. She paused for a moment, watching the clear water leap and rush, then took a few steps closer so that the whole scene opened up before her.

She caught her breath on seeing a figure sitting on a flat rock at the edge of the stream. The person was staring at the water, obviously lost in thought.

Dominique's heart lurched and she stifled a gasp as she suddenly recognised the dark hair just touching the collar of a white shirt.

It was Steve Daniels.

She took a step forward and her foot kicked a stone which tumbled down the slope and splashed into the stream.

Startled, Steve spun round, but when he saw who it was, his face broke into a smile that made her heart thud wildly.

Dominique felt a strange tingle charge through her body. That smile . . . those eyes . . . her legs shook and she couldn't deny the pleasure and excitement she felt at finding him there, in that idyllic place . . .

Steve Daniels was getting to his feet, and as she watched him, her heart beat so hard that it almost hurt. She hadn't experienced feelings like these since Tom.

She was further unnerved when she saw the expression in his eyes, the unmistakable admiration there. But she felt crushed because she knew how wrong it was for a nun to feel like this, distraught because his smile made her feel so wonderful . . .

He wasn't looking at her as a doctor would look at a nun, and he must see that her feelings were as transparent as his . . .

Steve continued to stare at her, unable to find the words he wanted to say. There was something about her face, the flush on her cheeks, the way her lips were parted. He looked into her eyes and what he saw there wasn't the chaste look of a nun.

The eyes that regarded him now were the passionate eyes of a woman filled with desire.

Dominique . . . ' Steve whispered as he got to his feet.

The initial surprise in his eyes was replaced by unreserved pleasure. He was as happy to see her, Dominique realised, as she was to see him.

He opened his arms as she drew

nearer and before she knew what had happened, she was enfolded within them — strong, powerful arms that held her so gently . . .

She could feel the warmth of his skin through the thin fabric of his shirt and, in the seconds that followed, every being in the forest seemed to stop and hold its breath.

The rushing of the water, the raucous song of a thousand birds, all faded until she could hear only the thunderous beating of his heart.

As she lifted her face to his, he saw that her cheeks were damp, but her tears were not those of sorrow, for her lips were turned upwards in a smile.

He lowered his head, slowly, almost cautiously at first, then, as their lips met, an explosion of feeling over-whelmed them both, as his arms around her tightened, and she returned his fierce embrace with equal passion.

At last he drew back and looked down at her, half expecting her to push him away.

But her eyes were still closed, sweeping dark lashes over her flushed cheeks. Her soft, full lips seemed to silently urge him to kiss her again.

This time, Dominique felt the last of her reservations disappear. At that moment there was no guilt, no remorse, just the certain knowledge that this was right.

It was only as they drew apart for the second time that the enormity of what had happened fully hit her.

She looked wonderingly at Steve. Joy and elation were running through her, but the fact remained that she was a nun.

To have merely contemplated these feelings went against her faith. To have given in to them so easily, was unforgivable . . .

Steve held her hand, raised it to his lips, watching her with mixed emotions as he kissed her fingers.

Dominique had come to him before and bared her soul, placing her trust in him completely.

Now he felt almost as though he were betraying that trust — yet he couldn't deny the deepening of his own feelings for her.

'Dominique.' He whispered her name, loving the very sound of it.

He wanted her so much . . . but suddenly reality hit him. They were alone in the forest, and soon it would be dark.

'We should be getting back,' he said softly, 'before we lose the last few minutes of daylight.'

Dominique nodded, unable to speak, so intense was her reaction to what had just happened between them.

Taking her hand in his, he led her towards the path which would take them out of the forest, pausing once to kiss her lightly on the lips.

'Forgive me, Dominique,' he murmured.

He didn't want to let her go, especially when it meant pretending that nothing had happened between them, but he had to. She was a nun. He had to keep reminding himself that.

Dominique's mind began to clear as they clambered up the path and through the tangled vines.

All the doubts of the last few months seemed to have culminated in those enchanted moments with Steve.

They walked on without uttering a word, eventually reaching the point in the forest where the two paths branched off — one to the waterfall, the other to the camp.

They both hesitated for a moment. Then, decisively, as if resisting further temptation, Steve began to lead them towards the camp.

Dominique had now to make a similar decision regarding her own future. Her own two paths had clearly reached a crossroads.

She could continue as a nun, bury herself in her faith and her work and refuse to give way to doubts and misgivings.

Or she could leave that life behind, return to the outside world . . .

She shivered. Leave the enclosed, ordered world of the Sisterhood? She'd never even thought of what that would be like.

Could she cope with the world and all its conflicting demands now?

Did she even want to? Somehow, she had always believed that her doubts would be overcome and resolved.

She looked up at Steve and he squeezed her hand and smiled at her, that wonderful, warm smile which made her heart turn over.

As they drew nearer to the camp, he released her hand and they deliberately walked apart.

Dominique bit hard on her lip, as she realised she must come to a decision about her future — soon.

★　★　★

Sister Magda caught sight of Sister Augusta swooping towards her like a huge black bird, her habit flowing out around her like massive wings. Her sharp eyes were fixed on Magda and the nun quailed inwardly, wondering what she had done to incur the Sister's wrath.

Then, surprisingly, Sister Augusta smiled. The gesture transformed her stern features and Magda sighed with relief.

'Sister Magda.' Sister Augusta crossed her arms and looked down at the younger nun. 'I want to talk to you.'

Almost without realising it, Magda's mind scanned the events of the past few days. What on earth could Sister Augusta want to speak to her about?

Normally the senior nun was up to her ears in administrative duties, with no time, or real inclination, for social niceties.

'I understand that you have successfully delivered a number of babies since your arrival.'

Magda nodded.

'And you have been conducting ante-natal classes?'

Again Magda nodded, wondering

where this was all leading. Sister Augusta's haughty look gave no indication.

'I also understand that you are trying to set up a clinic?'

'That's right, Sister . . . to educate young mothers, monitor the progress of their babies and children and to ensure that they are all properly immunised and so on,' Magda explained eagerly.

'Many of the young women living here have lost their own mothers, and grandmothers, in the earthquake, and those are the people they would normally go to for help and reassurance.

'There definitely is a need for such a scheme here, Sister Augusta.' Magda's face had lit up, taking on that familiar bloom of total commitment.

She was speaking with confidence, convinced she was right. Her only regret was that she wouldn't be able to stay on and watch her scheme take shape and grow.

'And you feel that it is within your

capabilities to initiate such a scheme?'

Magda's mouth went dry. So that was what this was all about. Sister Augusta was annoyed because Magda had taken it upon herself to start this scheme!

'I'm sorry, Sister.' She lowered her head. 'I realise I should have spoken to you first.'

Then she raised her chin with uncharacteristic defiance.

'But I knew how busy you were. You already have so much to do and, yes, I felt confident that, considering the experience I already have, I could do it on my own!'

'That's what I thought.' Sister Augusta's rigid expression relaxed and Magda was shocked to see what looked like relief in the older Sister's eyes.

'Much as I would like to,' Sister Augusta said with a sigh, 'I cannot see to everything. There is so much to organise with the rebuilding of the school, and the hospital, and now we must have a proper orphanage . . . '

Magda's spirits sank. Sister Augusta was endeavouring to say other things took priority over her infant care scheme. There were more important things to do.

'I have been speaking on the telephone to Reverend Mother General and she is of the same mind as me, Sister Magda.'

I'm going to be sent home, Magda thought miserably. After all this, I'm going to be sent home!

'We believe that it is in the best interests of everyone concerned if you stay on here, Sister Magda. But it is a hard and difficult decision I am asking you to make.

'The work will be exhausting and sometimes unrewarding.

'That is why we are not going to insist you stay here if you feel that you would rather return home. The fact is, I need someone like you, someone willing to take responsibility.

'Do you need time to consider?'

'No.' Magda shook her head. It was

impossible to keep from smiling, and her heart felt as if it was soaring right up into the sky.

'No, Sister, I don't need time to consider. My answer is yes. Yes, I would be happy to stay here!'

That night a full moon shone brightly from a clear sky, but inside the tent, it was not the light that was keeping Dominique awake.

Outside she could hear the high-pitched screeching of the insects, the scurrying of the creatures of the night as they went about their business. But they were not responsible for disturbing her sleep either.

Dominique turned over and looked despairingly at Magda, who was sleeping the sleep of the just. She couldn't help smiling.

Dear Magda, who had no doubts, who was content and happy. She had known from the start the direction her life should take and now her future was clearly mapped out before her.

Dominique turned away. If only her

own life could be as well-defined. Not that she resented Magda's contentment.

She had been overjoyed to learn that Magda would be staying on, and also a little sad because, in lots of ways, she would be losing a dear friend.

She sat up, and rested her chin on her knees.

Steve. Steve. Steve. She couldn't stop thinking about him.

When Tom had been killed, she had thought that falling in love could never happen again . . .

She felt herself shiver involuntarily when she recalled Steve taking her in his arms.

She pressed her fingers to her lips, remembering his soft, gentle kisses and how they'd made her feel so wonderful . . .

And then came the crushing weight of guilt. It was a vicious circle.

She couldn't sleep for thinking about Steve, but then those thoughts inevitably led her back to who she was — a nun, dedicated to the service of God, having knowingly and willingly turned her back on the wants and needs of womanhood.

She lay back down but, no matter how she tried, neither prayer nor sleep would come to her. Again and again her thoughts returned to Steve. When she closed her eyes, she saw his face. Smiling, blue eyes sparkling, dark hair flopping on to his forehead.

The easy stride with which he walked, the capable way he worked with the sick and injured. His gentleness with small, frightened children.

The way his hair just touched his collar. The way he held the hands of the dying . . .

Round and round. The night seemed endless. She could even hear his voice, soft, husky with desire.

She saw his big hands, long, artistic fingers working steadily to mend, repair and soothe. Big hands, but so gentle . . .

She sat up again. Would tonight ever

end? How could she sleep with these turbulent thoughts churning within her?

In despair, she lay back against the pillows, remembering her garden back at the English convent; trying to visualise her herb garden, she could almost feel the chill of a breeze as she harvested her crop.

Suddenly, for the first time in a long while, she was overcome with homesickness. She longed to smell the lavender, the sage; to see the gentle features of her Mother Superior.

And how would the head of the convent feel when she learned what Dominique had done, how she had betrayed her faith, her vows?

Yet no matter how she tried, Dominique couldn't bring herself to regret what had happened; and that was the hardest thing of all to come to terms with.

She should be devastated, filled with remorse, desperate for absolution, but she wasn't — she was ecstatically happy.

The tent was getting lighter. Soon it would be time to get up and Dominique hadn't slept at all. Soon she would have to face Father Gomez with her confession.

Now another feeling joined forces with all the rest to torment her. Shame. Despite her inner joy, she also felt deeply ashamed, and didn't know how she was ever going to confess about the time she'd spent with Steve in the forest.

9

After Mass, Dominique made straight for Father Gomez's tent. The camp was still relatively quiet as the nuns were normally up long before everyone else.

She hurried past the doctors' quarters, terrified in case she bumped into Steve. He was the last person she wanted to see right now, when her thoughts were already in such disarray.

Yet she would have loved to see him, too!

Father Gomez smiled in welcome as Dominique entered his tent. Then his smile became troubled.

She put her hand to her face. Surely her feelings weren't so obvious? Or was her guilt emblazoned on her face as clearly as it was etched into her heart?

The priest watched Dominique closely as she took her seat. Here was a troubled young woman — that much he'd known from the first time he'd listened to her confession.

He sighed and wondered what she had done — or thought she had done — this time. He remembered only too well how upset she had been following her confrontation with Esteban. She was so sensitive and caring . . .

But there was something else about her — a light in her eyes which hadn't been there before. A light that shone in the eyes of novices as they prepared to take their final vows, in the eyes of young women as they made their own, very different vows to the men they loved.

Could it be possible that Dominique had at last found peace? No, he decided. Not possible. Despite the brightness in her eyes, Dominique was still a deeply disturbed young woman.

But even Father Gomez, with all his experience, was not prepared for what was to come . . .

'When I reached the glade, I was already beginning to feel uplifted, more cheerful even . . . then I saw Steve, Dr Daniels, and when he turned and smiled at me . . . Oh, it's so hard to explain . . . '

At this point, she smiled herself and the light in her eyes shone even more brilliantly.

Father Gomez closed his eyes, and tried to compose his features so that his own feelings would not show. Then he looked directly at Dominique and waited for her to continue.

Dominique swallowed. She couldn't bring herself to go on, not yet. She stared down at her tightly-clenched hands.

How could she ever explain her true feelings to the priest? He couldn't begin to understand. His disappointment in her would be almost unbearable when he himself had placed such faith in her. How could she tell him?

She looked up and Father Gomez gently urged her to proceed.

'And . . . and then there was Pedro.' She smiled, remembering. 'That little boy has created more confusion in me than anyone! As I grew to love him, I suppose I saw the child I could never have as a nun.

'I miss Pedro desperately, Father . . . But Steve Daniels has reminded me of something else. He's reminded me that I'm still a woman.'

She drew in her breath and waited.

Father Gomez still looked impassive and she wondered if he really was unshockable.

'When we met in the forest, I forgot everything. Forgot that I was a nun . . . Father, when Steve took me in his arms and kissed me, I welcomed his embrace.

'I did nothing to prevent it happening, although I know I could have done.

'I just know that since it happened, I haven't thought of anything else but him. I'm filled with love for him, yet at the same time, I know it's completely wrong for me to feel this way.'

She finished abruptly. There was nothing else to say — apart from the fact she was sorry. Sorry, but not in the way she should be . . .

Father Gomez looked at her searchingly and Dominique waited nervously for his reaction, clasping and unclasping her hands on her lap.

The silence went on. An old battered clock, rescued from the rubble of the Father's old house, ticked loudly as if to remind them that time was passing quickly.

Dominique felt her heart beat faster. Was the Father so displeased with her that he couldn't bring himself to speak?

At last, after several minutes consideration, Father Gomez shifted in his chair. He leaned forward and Dominique looked up, meeting his gaze, ready to accept whatever he told her.

'You have been searching for an answer,' he said and his tone was matter-of-fact. 'Sister Dominique, what more do you want as a sign?'

She gasped, still not fully understanding.

'I think God has spoken very clearly

to you — if only you will open your heart and listen to what He is telling you. You do still believe in God's infinite wisdom and love, don't you?'

'Oh, yes, I do, Father.' Dominique spoke passionately. 'Strange as it sounds, in the last few days I feel as though I've come closer to Him.

'It's as if lately I've been out of touch with Him. I felt that He wasn't listening to me, but, perhaps, Father, it was I who wasn't listening.'

Her face was flushed — every word she spoke was coming straight from her heart.

Father Gomez knew now what he had to tell her.

'I think God has made your way ahead very clear. Your place may not be with the Sisterhood, but there are many other ways in which you may serve and love Him. Vows have been broken, Sister. There will be criticism, accusation . . . but not from me.

'How can it ever be wrong to love another person? God loves us all and

He wants us to love each other. In your case, you have come to love one man above all others — and Steve Daniels is a good, kind, caring man.

'But, Sister, that doesn't mean you love God any less.'

Father Gomez's voice grew more fervent, charged as it was with such conviction.

'In your short time with us, you've done so much good. Despite your own worries, you have given yourself wholly to these people. Caring for the wounded and dying, comforting the bereaved, loving the little children who needed affection and a kind word.

'You've given people hope. Like young Esteban. You reached him where so many of us had failed and gave him the courage to start rebuilding his life and begin to trust in God again.

'As for Pedro, you have the strength, out of real love, to see a little boy you adored go to the parents who so desperately needed and wanted him.'

Dominique's throat felt dry and tears

stung her tired eyes. She had come here expecting to be on the receiving end of bitter words and harsh judgement. Instead, Father Gomez was showing her nothing but compassion and understanding.

He was a remarkable man.

'Never, never underestimate yourself or the valuable work that you have already carried out in your service to God.

'You're a good woman, Sister Dominique, with the potential to give and receive so much love. I am not going to tell you what to do, that is something you must inevitably decide for yourself, but you can be assured of God's help and guidance.

'God go with you, Sister.'

The gentle, softly-spoken words filled Dominique's heart. She had come to this place with so many unanswered questions. Now her way forward was clear — no more ifs, no more buts . . .

Then suddenly her tranquillity was shattered by one final, devastating thought . . .

She and Steve had become friends.

They had shared a moment of mutual attraction . . .

But what if his feelings ran no deeper than that?

★   ★   ★

Sister Magda looked around her small class of expectant mothers and smiled. She'd never thought she could be so happy.

It warmed her heart to see these women who'd endured so much in the recent past, looking ahead again with hope. If all went well, Magda — who'd helped with courses on nutrition and ante-natal exercises — would soon be helping to bring their babies into the world.

Even though she'd been present at many births, each one was still a special miracle to the young nun.

She dismissed the class, still smiling serenely.

'There's someone to see you, Sister Magda,' one of the nurses from the hospital said when the mothers-to-be had gone. 'He's waiting outside.'

'I'll be right out.' Magda shuffled her papers together tidily and pushed them into her bag.

Her smile quickly faded when she emerged from the tent. There was something familiar about the young man waiting to see her.

She peered at him through the bright sunlight. He was young, but had those sad eyes that so many people seemed to have since the disaster.

'Can I help you?' she asked.

'Sister Magda, I am Esteban,' he said hesitantly.

'Esteban,' she whispered. Dominique had spoken frequently of her concern for him and Magda remembered seeing him around the camp. He'd always seemed dirty and dishevelled and angry — so very angry.

He had been drunk most of the time, and abusive. No-one had any time for him; no-one except Father Gomez and Dominique.

Dominique had taken him to task, Magda remembered, and Father Gomez had been delighted because it had really seemed to do the trick.

Sister Magda realised it was true. She had never seen such a complete and utter transformation.

The young man's clothes had seen better days, but they were clean and he had obviously made an effort to appear presentable.

He grinned, flashing white teeth, and Magda relaxed. The Esteban she had seen and secretly feared had gone.

This quiet, unassuming, sad young man was, she suspected, the true Esteban, the one who had been lost for a while after his bride's tragic death in the earthquake.

'I have seen Sister Augusta,' he mumbled. 'She says you are planning to run a clinic for the mothers and babies.'

'That's right,' Magda nodded. She still couldn't believe that it was true.

'You will need help with the building work,' he went on. 'I would like to volunteer . . . if you'll have me.'

'Your help would be very welcome, Esteban.' Magda smiled broadly. He was her first volunteer, the first of many she felt sure, but even if he was the only one, she would still build her clinic — somehow.

'God bless you.' She turned and walked away and Esteban watched her go, a sad smile on his lips. He still missed his wife, still felt angry, but, in a strange way, he was coming to terms with it . . .

Dominique stood in the entrance to the hospital tent, remembering how she had felt on the day of her arrival. Then, it had been crammed full of emergency cases.

She would never forget Pedro's appealing little face watching her from behind a curtain, hiding away when she turned to look at him.

Even now she smiled and felt a delicious warmth surge through her as she remembered his small hand stealing into her own.

Now, the hospital, although far from ideal, was no longer cramped. Most of the patients were there only for routine treatment.

She moved forward, ready to begin her day's work. At the far end of the tent, she caught a glimpse of Steve Daniels and abruptly turned the other way.

She couldn't see him yet! She wasn't ready.

'Hello, Nina.' She hurried to the bed of a small girl. 'How are you?'

'I'm going home today.' The child grinned, displaying her gappy teeth.

'That's wonderful news. I bet you're looking forward to it.' Dominique gently slipped a thermometer into Nina's mouth and held her wrist to take her pulse. She allowed her jumbled thoughts to stray for just a few moments.

What would she say when she saw Steve? Should she tell him how she felt about him? She hadn't felt so alive and happy in years . . .

She took out the thermometer, read

it, then smiled at little Nina.

'Good. Your temperature's normal!' She wrote the appropriate figures on the chart at the end of the child's bed. 'Don't forget to come and say goodbye before you go!'

Continuing along the ward, Dominique took temperatures, read blood pressures, chatted to and reassured her patients. It was all very routine, but never dull.

'You look different, Sister,' an old lady, one of the remaining casualties from the earthquake, observed.

'Different, Blanca?' Dominique smiled. 'How do you mean?'

Blanca smiled and shrugged. She was maybe old but she was a sharp as a needle.

'If it wasn't wicked of me to say so, I'd say you were in love!'

'Then don't say it!' Dominique quipped back quickly. 'It is wicked!'

The old woman cackled loudly and Dominique blushed. Were her feelings so obvious? She hoped not.

After years of prayer and selfless devotion to God, being in love felt strange and wrong, yet new and exciting.

She coaxed a male patient from his bed, urging him to take a few steps along the ward. The atmosphere was tense. Everyone fell silent as Dominique spoke her soothing words.

'Come along, Rodolfo,' she whispered encouragingly. 'Everyone's watching you! Don't let them down. You can do it!'

The determination firing Dominique seemed to rub off on Rodolfo.

Clinging tightly to her arm, he took six unsteady steps. Dominique's smile was triumphant as all the patients cheered.

'Keep it up,' Dominique told him, 'and you'll walk out of this place in ten days!'

Triumphs like this happened every day, as did setbacks. She had learned to rejoice in the triumphs, to overcome the setbacks. If only she could use that philosophy in her personal life!

There was Steve again, at the far end of the ward. He looked busy. She moved along to the next patient.

Then she knew why she was avoiding him. Realisation hit her sharply. She didn't doubt the strength of her feelings for him, but what about his feelings for her?

What if he didn't love her? What if that moment in the forest had been no more than one of intense physical attraction for him?

Relentlessly, the same questions and doubts whirled round and round in her head.

The morning seemed to drag by. She tended conscientiously to her patients, aware of her drifting thoughts and eager to compensate for them.

She was willing to renounce the Sisterhood for the love of this man, go anywhere for him, but what was there to say that he loved her enough to make sacrifices for her?

She remembered the way he'd looked at her, the desire in his eyes, the tenderness of his voice when he spoke her name . . . his kisses; those wonderful passionate moments together surely meant as much to him.

Dominique had no control over her turbulent thoughts as they swung backwards and forwards.

She loved him — she was certain of that. But did he love her? It was the same question, over and over again, and it was one she could not answer . . .

10

Steve looked down at the little boy lying on the bed. He had split his head after falling in the street.

It was only a small gash, but the boy's mother was distraught. She'd lost her two other children in the earthquake and so he could well appreciate her panic when her youngest child was hurt. The woman continued to weep as a nurse tried to comfort her and explain that her son's injury looked worse than it was.

Steve wished fervently that Dominique was with him. She would know how to speak to her in Spanish and to calm her. But Dominique was busy.

He'd looked over at her several times and she always seemed occupied.

The thought occurred to him that she might be trying to avoid him and he couldn't blame her.

The child stirred restlessly and Steve turned to the anxious mother.

'Just hold his hand. He'll be all right,' he said, hoping she could understand from his tone of voice that there was no need to worry.

Then she looked down at her son, squeezed his hand and smiled. 'Gracias.'

And the child lay still as Steve neatly stitched the wound, his thoughts straying again to Dominique.

Falling in love had been the last thing on his mind. He had his work — that was his special relationship. He never saw himself as the type of man who would be happy to settle down and get married, although he'd known plenty of beautiful, intelligent women.

Like Lisa Wayne. She'd been attractive, and witty, and was a skilled doctor, and she'd been very much in love with him. But for some reason it hadn't felt right.

There hadn't been that spark between them. He'd often wondered in the past if it was him . . . if he expected too much from relationships, always searching for that apparently inexplicable chemistry.

Yet yesterday, with Dominique, he had been proved wrong. Sparks had flown, the chemistry had been right. That elusive element everyone talked about and which he had been waiting for all his life had crept up and taken him completely unawares!

He lifted the little boy down from the bed and grinned at him. 'You're a very brave boy,' he said. 'Come back to the hospital in a week and we'll take those stitches out and you'll be as good as new!'

Then he turned to the little boy's mother and patted her arm and smiled reassuringly.

With the departure of his last patient, his thoughts turned again to Dominique.

He had hardly slept last night, all because he couldn't stop thinking about her.

She was so different to anyone he'd

ever known before. Despite the fact that she'd once been married, there was a curious innocence about her, a youthful freshness which was so appealing.

Yesterday's events had taken him completely by surprise. It was a wonderful feeling . . . but it didn't alter the fact that Dominique was a nun!

She had confided in him, told him of her uncertainties. Perhaps she would think that he had deliberately taken advantage of her, knowing how vulnerable she was.

Would she ever believe that his feelings had been growing since . . . since . . . He didn't know himself. Whether they had grown out of admiration for her dedication, or from that first walk they'd taken together in the forest when they had discovered a mutual love of nature, he couldn't say. Still deep in his own thoughts, he went through to the ante-room to check his schedule for the next day.

Dominique always liked to see the schedules for the next day, too. If she was going to be assisting in theatre, then she'd have to make an effort to get some rest. She walked quickly down the ward, saying good-night to the patients as she went. Off duty, she would perhaps be able to get her tormented thoughts enough in order to secure a night's sleep — and to make up her mind exactly what she was going to say to him. Because one way or another it had to be sorted out.

Pushing the flap aside, she walked into the ante-room and cannoned into Steve Daniels, who was on his way out.

Startled, each took a step backwards, both opened their mouths to speak at once, but both were lost for words.

All those carefully rehearsed speeches were lost to Dominique as she looked up at him. What was he thinking? Was it that she'd made more of that unforgettable moment in the forest than he?

Steve was going through the same doubts, but wanting so much to believe, from her expression, that she felt as he did.

Eventually, after a silence which seemed interminable, Steve blurted out, 'I've been thinking about you all day, Dominique. I can't get you out of my mind.' Dominique looked him straight in the eye, knowing now exactly which path she was going to follow.

Her voice was soft, but sincere. 'I feel the same way, Steve. I love you . . . ' and she slipped quite naturally into his waiting arms.

★　★　★

A family of blackbirds suddenly appeared on the lawn. Mother, father and three youngsters. The young woman looked up from the letter she was reading as the three fledglings flapped for attention and demanded food from their tireless parents.

The baby inside her stirred. She placed her hand on her swollen abdomen and her smile was radiant when she was rewarded by tiny, fluttering movements.

She looked around her at the beautiful garden, the birds accentuating the tranquillity and peace of the place with their song.

She was waiting in the convent garden for Steve to come and collect her.

They'd been on holiday in England and Dominique was taking this chance to renew old acquaintances and to say final farewells, before they returned home. In less than two hours, they'd be on a plane bound for America, where they now lived.

The breeze ruffled the letter in her hands and she looked back again at the childish scrawl, where she had left off.

She could almost hear little Pedro's voice as she read his words.

I love Luis and Dorotea very much. They have been very kind to me, Sister, and I am very happy, just as you said I would be.

I am top in my class in story writing and drawing and I go to school every day. I promise I never skip lessons. I draw you.

Here there was a gap in the text where Pedro had sketched Dominique as he remembered her. Not in her everyday nurse's clothes, but in the habit she had been wearing when she first arrived at the camp.

She laughed out loud, startling the birds on the lawn. Was that really how Pedro saw her? No wonder he'd kept staring at her on that first day!

I went back to the camp to see my friends and Father Gomez. The church is almost finished now and there is a new hospital and a school. It is like a different place, but just the same.

I saw Sister Magda. She is always smiling. I like her. She says she will always be grateful to God for letting her stay with the people she loves so much.

Dominique owed her own debt of gratitude to God and the Church — for releasing her from her vows and allowing her to follow her chosen path.

She could picture Magda as clearly as if she were hurrying across the lawn towards her and she was so pleased that things had worked out for her.

They had both found peace and happiness, but in such different ways.

Esteban is her biggest helper, the letter continued. Dominique raised her eyebrows in surprise. She felt a tremor of pride. He was a good man and she prayed that one day he, too, would find happiness again.

Esteban sends his regards to you, Sister Dominique. He says 'Mucha suerte!'

Again Dominique laughed out loud. How she loved and missed them all! And how sweet of Esteban to remember her and wish her good luck.

Do you still have the watch I gave to you? Does it keep good time?

She glanced down at it and nodded.

'Yes, Pedro,' she whispered. 'It keeps very good time.'

She remembered still, with a stab of guilt, how she had accused him of stealing it, how she had hurt him. She wondered, too, how Chuck, the ever-cheerful GI had fared since he had gone home. Well, she hoped. He deserved happiness.

Steve would be here soon. She folded the letter carefully and slipped it into her bag.

Contentedly, she sat on the bench seat, looking around at the beautiful garden. Flowers bloomed in profusion, the fragrance of honeysuckle mingled with the heady scent of the rose garden.

Once, Dominique had lovingly tended those flowers, gathered these herbs. Now the task and the joy belonged to another.

Her new contentment filled her with serenity and there, in the simple beauty of the garden, she felt compelled to offer a prayer of thanks.

Since falling in love with Steve, she had no doubt that God had been guiding her in every move she made; by leading her to that faraway country; for teaching her so much about human frailty and fortitude and finally for restoring her faith in people and in His church.

Just as she'd finished thanking God

for these blessings, she heard the huge gate at the end of the convent garden creak open and Steve walked through.

Her heart turned over and she couldn't help but smile as he crossed towards her, with his long, easy stride.

Feeling an overwhelming surge of love for her husband, she hurried to greet him. He hugged her happily.

He'd been concerned that coming back to the convent would unsettle her, even rekindle her old doubts and worries, but, if anything, it had strengthened her.

He hugged her again, then arm in arm they headed back towards the ornate gate.

Dominique turned for one last look at the garden she had once looked upon as her own.

Her attention was caught as a young nun emerged from the building. The girl wore an apron over her habit and Dominique watched as she kneeled and began to work among the herbs.

Standing at the window of her office,

the Mother Superior became aware of another presence in the room and turned to see Sister Bernadette, the Mistress of Novices, hovering in the doorway.

'Come in, come in,' she called warmly, looking back over her shoulder through the open window. She had been watching Dominique, but as the former nun disappeared for the last time through the gate, her gaze strayed to the young nun now toiling in the garden.

Sister Bernadette moved over to the window to join her Reverend Mother. It was a glorious day, and the garden was looking at its best.

'How lovely it was to see Sister Dominique again — and to know that she is truly happy at last, serving God in her own way.'

The Mother Superior smiled as she spoke. Dominique would have beautiful babies and each would be a testament to her final decision to leave the Sisterhood.

She turned to look at Sister Bernadette. The Mistress of Novices was looking wistful.

It was always sad when they lost one of their own, but they couldn't be sad about Dominique. Not when she was so obviously happy and content with her new life.

The head of the convent sighed. 'To think I sent two of my nuns out there and neither of them came back to me as I expected! Yet I can't help feeling pleased for them both. Dominique will be a good wife and mother, of that I have no doubts.

'As for Sister Magda, she has enough dedication for a dozen Sisters! Already she has done so much good. She is an inspiration to us all!

'So much changes, and yet . . . '

She looked affectionately at her Mistress of Novices. Sister Bernadette was as crumpled as ever, but she had always been more concerned with the welfare of her novices than with her own appearance.

It was not a fault, but a virtue!

The Mother Superior turned back to the window. The novice in the garden was working with a passion she hadn't seen since Dominique's time here.

'Yet so much remains the same . . . ' She pointed at the young novice down in the garden to illustrate her point as she moved away from the window and sat down at her desk.

Sister Bernadette cleared her throat.

'In fact, Mother, that's why I'm here.' She looked down at the garden, then back at the Mother Superior. 'I wanted to have a word with you about Sister Angelina. She's been to see me . . . ' She broke off, looking close to despair.

'Apparently she's been having some doubts about her calling . . . '

Mother Katherine raised her eyes towards the ceiling as Sister Bernadette sat down opposite.

'Well, Sister Bernadette,' she said at last with a sigh, the merest smile playing on her lips, 'isn't that what life is all about?'

We do hope that you have enjoyed reading this large print book.

Did you know that all of our titles are available for purchase?

We publish a wide range of high quality large print books including:
Romances, Mysteries, Classics
General Fiction
Non Fiction and Westerns

Special interest titles available in large print are:
The Little Oxford Dictionary
Music Book, Song Book
Hymn Book, Service Book

Also available from us courtesy of Oxford University Press:
Young Readers' Dictionary
(large print edition)
Young Readers' Thesaurus
(large print edition)

For further information or a free brochure, please contact us at:
Ulverscroft Large Print Books Ltd.,
The Green, Bradgate Road, Anstey,
Leicester, LE7 7FU, England.
Tel: (00 44) 0116 236 4325
Fax: (00 44) 0116 234 0205

Other titles in the
Linford Romance Library:

AN UNEXPECTED ENCOUNTER

Fenella Miller

Miss Victoria Marsh has an unexpected encounter in the church with a handsome, but disagreeable, soldier who is recuperating from a grievous leg injury. Major Toby Highcliff believes himself to be a useless cripple, but meeting Victoria changes everything. Will he be able to keep her safe from the evil that stalks the neighbourhood and convince her he is the ideal man for her?